"You need me." A g[...] Lauren's face. "What a perfectly lovely position for me to be in."

"Don't get too cocky, sweetheart. There are other people in the world who have a way with fractious horses."

"Maybe so, but none of them are me. Nor are they here. Right now, I'm all you've got." Lauren reached up and patted Wade's cheek. "Be nice to me."

The touch was no more than a two-second caress, but Wade's pulse took off. The woman was a sorceress. At this rate, she'd have him tamed right along with Midnight. He couldn't have that.

Before she could tuck her hand safely beneath the table, he caught it in midair and brought it to his lips. Gaze clashing with hers, he kissed her knuckles.

"A word of warning," he murmured.

"What?" she whispered, her voice suddenly shaky.

"You don't want to play with fire."

Dear Reader,

Around this time of year, everyone reflects on what it is that they're thankful for. For reader favorite Susan Mallery, the friendships she's made since becoming a writer have made a difference in her life. Bestselling author Sherryl Woods is thankful for the letters from readers—"It means so much to know that a particular story has touched someone's soul." And popular author Janis Reams Hudson is thankful "for the readers who spend their hard-earned money to buy my books."

I'm thankful to have such a talented group of writers in the Silhouette Special Edition line, and the authors appearing this month are no exception! In *Wrangling the Redhead* by Sherryl Woods, find out if the heroine's celebrity status gets in the way of true love.… Also don't miss *The Sheik and the Runaway Princess* by Susan Mallery, in which the Prince of Thieves kidnaps a princess…and simultaneously steals her heart!

When the heroine claims her late sister's child, she finds the child's guardian—and possibly the perfect man—in *Baby Be Mine* by Victoria Pade. And when a handsome horse breeder turns out to be a spy enlisted to expose the next heiress to the Haskell fortune, will he find an impostor or the real McCoy in *The Missing Heir* by Jane Toombs? In Ann Roth's *Father of the Year,* should this single dad keep his new nanny…or make her his wife? And the sparks fly when a man discovers his secret baby daughter left on his doorstep…which leads to a marriage of convenience in Janis Reams Hudson's *Daughter on His Doorstep.*

I hope you enjoy all these wonderful novels by some of the most talented authors in the genre. Best wishes to you and your family for a very happy and healthy Thanksgiving!

Best,

Karen Taylor Richman
Senior Editor

Please address questions and book requests to:
Silhouette Reader Service
U.S.: 3010 Walden Ave., P.O. Box 1325, Buffalo, NY 14269
Canadian: P.O. Box 609, Fort Erie, Ont. L2A 5X3

Sherryl Woods

Wrangling the Redhead

Silhouette

SPECIAL EDITION™

Published by Silhouette Books

America's Publisher of Contemporary Romance

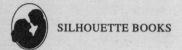 **SILHOUETTE BOOKS**

ISBN 0-373-24429-0

WRANGLING THE REDHEAD

Copyright © 2001 by Sherryl Woods

This edition published by arrangement with Harlequin Books S.A.

® and TM are trademarks of Harlequin Books S.A., used under license.
Trademarks indicated with ® are registered in the United States Patent
and Trademark Office, the Canadian Trade Marks Office and in other
countries.

Visit Silhouette at www.eHarlequin.com

Printed in U.S.A.

Books by Sherryl Woods

SHERRYL WOODS

has written more than seventy-five novels. She also operates her own bookstore, Potomac Sunrise, in Colonial Beach, Virginia. If you can't visit Sherryl at her store, then be sure to drop her a note at P.O. Box 490326, Key Biscayne, FL 33149 or check out her Web site at www.sherrylwoods.com.

Winding River High School
Class of '91

Welcome Home——Ten Years Later
Do You Remember the Way We Were?

Lauren Winters — The girl with all the answers, otherwise known as the one you'd most like to be seated next to during an exam. Elected most likely to succeed. Class valedictorian. Member of the Honor Society, County Fair Junior Rodeo Queen and star of the junior and senior class plays.

Emma Rogers — That girl can swing...a bat, that is. Elected most likely to be the first female on the New York Yankees. Member of the Debate Club, the Honor Society and president of the senior class.

Gina Petrillo — Tastiest girl in the class. Elected most popular because nobody in town bakes a better double chocolate brownie. Member of the Future Homemakers of America. Winner of three blue ribbons in the pie-baking contest and four in the cake-baking contest at the county fair.

Cassie Collins — Ringleader of the Calamity Janes. Elected most likely to land in jail. Best known for painting the town water tower a shocking pink and for making the entire faculty regret choosing teaching as a profession. Class record for detentions.

Karen (Phipps) Hanson — Better known as The Dreamer. Elected most likely to see the world. Member of the 4-H club, the Spanish and French clubs, and first-place winner at the county fair greased pig contest.

Prologue

The plastic surgeon, a Hollywood celebrity in his own right, seemed particularly enamored by his computerized demonstration of exactly what he could achieve with a face-lift.

"A little nip right here," he said, clicking a key and altering the world-famous face on the screen so that the already flawless skin around the eyes was an almost imperceptible smidgen tighter. "A tuck here." The soft, rounded chin disappeared.

"It'll take ten years off," he promised enthusiastically. "And now's the time to start, before the aging process really gets a grip on you."

Lauren Winters listened to his spiel, stared at the image of her face on the screen and shuddered.

What was she thinking? She was only twenty-eight, and she was worrying about taking ten years off of her appearance. Was she suddenly expecting to be cast in some teen flick as an eighteen-year-old high-school senior? Hardly. She was doing just fine playing leading ladies her own age in blockbuster romantic comedies.

Making this appointment to discuss plastic surgery had obviously been a knee-jerk reaction to her latest divorce. That made two failed marriages—not bad by Hollywood standards, but a far cry from what she'd anticipated when she'd been growing up on a ranch in Winding River, Wyoming, where marriages—even bad ones like her parents'—tended to last forever.

Suddenly her life seemed incredibly shallow and pointless. Mentally she ticked off the accomplishments and their downside.

Her marriages had been career moves...for the men.

She had made more money than she'd ever dreamed of, but had no one to spend it on, since her parents refused to take a dime from her. They had only recently agreed to sell their failing ranch, put the money into savings and use the winter retreat Lauren had bought for them in Arizona. Her father grumbled about it every single time they spoke. He acted as if her gift were a banishment, rather than a generous gesture.

Her picture was on the cover of magazines...the kind no one in her family read.

She'd starred in five box office smashes in a row, though few people in Winding River ever made the trip to Laramie to see them, although some later rented the videos. Her old neighbors considered a night of dancing at the Heartbreak or dinner at Stella's or Tony's to be the height of entertainment. They were proud of her, but only in an abstract sort of way. Some actually seemed a little vague about what it was she did.

Even so, she was, by any standard, a successful, accomplished actress, but Lauren could honestly say she had no idea who she was anymore.

The invitation to her tenth high-school reunion had reminded her of that. A personal note from the class president had gushed on and on about Lauren's Hollywood acclaim and said nothing at all about the teenage girl she'd been. Heck, back then, they'd barely spoken, which said volumes about how fame managed to turn former acquaintances into lifelong friends. Mimi Frances seemed to know Lauren Winters, superstar, better than Lauren knew herself.

Lauren had never felt comfortable in the role of actress, much less superstar. It seemed as fake to her as the fictional characters she played on-screen. There were a half-dozen identities that seemed more fitting and familiar: Lauren Winters, straight-A student; Lauren Winters, class valedictorian; Lauren Winters, president of the debate team; Lauren Winters, best friend; Lauren Winters, horse trainer; Lauren Winters, bookkeeper. Those were the parts of her that counted for something. They were the achievements she could point to with pride.

And, she realized with sudden clarity, she wanted them back. Okay, maybe not the bookkeeping, but the rest of it, the friendships and the horses and the respect for her brain as opposed to her beauty. She wanted to go home and find the old Lauren, who'd never even set foot in front of a camera, much less dreamed of being an actress.

Most of all, she wanted to see the Calamity Janes, her four best friends. The five of them had stuck together through thick and thin, stayed up all night talking about boys and dreams and spent hours on end creating mischief that had kept the whole town talking.

Even now, Lauren reflected, Cassie, Karen, Emma and Gina kept her grounded, though they were scattered around the country and phone calls were all that kept them connected. Nonetheless, they were always there with a shoulder to cry on, advice and, most of all, laughter. They were the people who mattered, not the agents and managers and publicists whose fortunes rose and fell with hers, not the men who sought the spotlight by being photographed at her side.

Her life these last ten years seemed more like an incredible fluke than something she'd achieved through hard work and ambition. Being discovered by a producer after she'd only been on the job in his studio accountant's office for a month was the stuff of Hollywood legends. She'd laughed when he'd asked her to audition for his latest movie. She'd considered it a lark when she'd gotten the small but pivotal role that had ultimately earned her an Academy Award nomination.

But that nomination had made it all but impossible for her to go back to being an anonymous bookkeeper, whose success depended solely on whether the numbers added up at the end of the year. Other directors had taken her seriously, sought her out. The roles had kept coming, right along with the recognition and the publicity and the men. In what seemed like the blink of an eye, she'd become a sought-after superstar.

And along the way, *she* had gotten lost.

The doctor's voice snapped her back to the present.

"So, Ms. Winters, shall I have my assistant schedule you for surgery next week? My calendar is booked months ahead, but for you I'm sure we can find some time." The doctor beamed at her, his capped teeth gleaming, as he granted what he obviously viewed as a huge favor, though they both knew that having her for a client would be a publicity coup for him. He promised total discretion, but word would leak out. It always did.

Lauren weighed her choices—taking a trip home to see her best friends for their class reunion or having this ridiculously vain and unnecessary bit of surgery. In the end, there was no contest.

"Thank you so much for your time, Doctor, but I think I like my face just the way it is. I'll keep it a while longer," she said.

He stared at her, clearly stunned. "But if you wait, I can't guarantee that the results will be as good."

She gave him one of her trademark brilliant smiles, the one that had most men stumbling over their own feet. "To tell you the truth, Doctor, I don't think the horses and cattle in Winding River will care."

Chapter One

This week the Calamity Janes had gathered around Karen's kitchen table for their Monday-night get-together. Now that Emma had moved back from Denver and opened her law practice, now that Gina was taking over Tony's Italian restaurant in Winding River and Cassie had settled into her marriage with Cole, they assembled someplace each week to discuss their lives. Lauren joined them whenever she could, which was more and more frequently of late.

Even when she wasn't in town, she had a feeling she was a prime topic of conversation. They were openly worried about her. She was the only one of them who hadn't moved home again in the months since their class reunion had first brought her home. She was also the only one of them not happily married or engaged. Maybe if she'd been bubbling with enthusiasm for her life in Los Angeles, they wouldn't be so concerned, but Lauren hadn't been able to hide her disenchantment.

That being the case, not even she could explain why she hadn't made the decision to move back to Winding River, when it was apparently clear to everyone that Los Angeles no longer held the allure it once had.

She stood for a moment on the back steps at the Blackhawk ranch that had become her home away from home, listening to the low hum of conversation inside, breathing in the soft, spring air, staring up at the clear, star-studded sky. This was the only place on earth where she felt totally at peace. Over the last few months she had finally begun to find herself again. Now she just had to reconcile what she was discovering with the life she'd been leading for the last ten years.

She heard her name mentioned, along with an increasingly familiar refrain, and knew that any private soul-searching was over for now.

"I'm telling you, something is seriously wrong. Lauren isn't happy. I know she wants to move back," Karen said for what had to be the thousandth time. "We have to do something."

Lauren sighed, knocked on the screen door, then entered without waiting for a response.

"Talking about me behind my back again?" she asked lightly as she pulled out a chair and joined them. "Or did you know I was just outside?"

"I'd say the same thing to your face," Karen retorted, obviously not the least bit embarrassed at having been caught. "In fact, I've been saying it so often, even *I'm* tired of hearing it."

"Then why not drop it?" Lauren asked, unable to keep the edge out of her voice. The well-meant pressure wasn't helping her to make up her mind. If anything, it was complicating the decision, making her wonder in the wee hours of the night if she wanted to come home for herself or because it was what her friends wanted. Would she be running *from* something or to something?

"I won't drop it, because you're not happy," Karen said, frowning at her. "And I don't know why you won't do something to fix it."

Emma stared at Lauren over the rim of her coffee cup. "Is Karen right? Do you want to move back? We've all heard you making noises about it for months now. What's the holdup? Stop second-guessing yourself. Just do it…if it's what you really want."

"You're here half the time anyway," Cassie pointed out. "Why not make it official?"

They were right, Lauren acknowledged silently. If it *was* what she wanted, what she'd been alluding to ever since their reunion, it was time to act. One by one, her friends had come back home to Winding River. They were happy here. They'd found something that had been missing from their lives. She envied them that more than she could say.

But what if she didn't find the same kind of contentment? What if she was romanticizing all of this? What if she was imagining that she'd be happier living a normal life in Wyoming than she was being in the center of a glamorous whirlwind in Hollywood? What if she burned her bridges and came home…only to discover that she was just as miserable? What if the problem was something inside her and not her career at all? Was she ready to risk making such a terrible discovery about herself?

"Talk to us," Gina nudged. "Why are you hesitating?"

"It's a huge step," Lauren said, hedging because she didn't fully understand her hesitation herself.

Emma nodded. "Okay, but what are the risks? It's not the money. Unless you've been extremely foolish, you should have enough stashed away to last a lifetime."

"True," Lauren agreed. Leave it to the ever-focused Emma to begin reducing the decision to a list of pros and cons.

"And you're not that crazy about being recognized everywhere you go," Cassie weighed in. "So it can't be that you'll miss that."

"Absolutely not," Lauren said fervently. She hated having strangers watching her every move, taking note of it, even reporting it to some tabloid.

"Is it the acting?" Karen asked. "I've always had the feeling that you don't take it all that seriously, even though you do it well. Am I wrong? Do you think you'll miss it?"

Lauren shook her head. "It's not the acting. It's fun, but it doesn't really mean anything to me. I'm not driven to perform."

"What about all the hunky men? Is that it?" Gina asked, grinning. "Goodness knows, we'd all miss hearing about them, but I'm willing to sacrifice all those titillating inside stories to have you home."

Lauren shuddered. "It is definitely *not* the men. Been there, done that. I haven't met a one who wasn't totally self-absorbed."

"What, then?" Emma asked. "Give us one reason why moving back here to be close to all of us wouldn't be the smartest thing you've ever done?"

Cassie nudged Emma with an elbow. "Could be you hit it on the head," she teased. "We're all here to bug her to death until she finds someone and settles down like the rest of us. That could be annoying.''

"Us? Annoying?'' Emma said with exaggerated shock.

Lauren grinned. ''Yes, well, there is that. You are a bunch of know-it-alls.''

"We'll make a vow,'' Emma said, looking pious. ''You can make all your own decisions. We'll stay out of everything.''

"Like you're staying out of this?'' Lauren taunted.

"Well, *after* this,'' Emma replied blithely. ''We have a vested interest in your return. We want you nearby. Our kids want you nearby. You spoil them all shamelessly.''

Lauren had been on the verge of making the decision to move back to Winding River for a long time now. She'd practically made a nuisance of herself by dropping in to stay with Karen at the blink of an eye. For a while she'd been able to claim that she was helping Karen out after her husband had died, but in the weeks since Karen had married Grady Blackhawk and moved to his ranch, which was closer to Winding River than her first husband's, Lauren had continued to visit. She hadn't even felt the need to come up with a new excuse. She just kept appearing on Karen and Grady's doorstep. She had an entire wardrobe stashed in their guest room.

Grady had been amazingly tolerant about it. Because he was so completely and totally smitten with his new wife, he was one of the few men whose jaw didn't drop when he looked at Lauren. She liked that about him. He treated her like a worthwhile human being, not a means to an end. Emma's husband, Ford, was the same way, as were Cassie's Cole and Gina's Rafe. It was nice to be around males who were real, who respected her mind, not just her looks.

Maybe that was part of the problem. She was comfortable as a guest in the Blackhawk home. If she moved back, she'd have to find her own place, build her own life, not live on the periphery of theirs. It was a scary prospect. What on earth would she do here if she came back? She had too much energy to simply retire, even though she could well afford to do so. And doing bookkeeping, which had been her ticket out of Winding River, would bore her to tears now.

Karen reached across the table and squeezed her hand. "It's time, sweetie. Just bite the bullet and do it. You can stay right here with Grady and me for as long as you want. In fact, he'd love it if you helped out with the horses. The new wrangler he hired last week is fantastic, but Grady says nobody has your touch."

"Are you serious?" Lauren asked, feeling a little surge of excitement in the pit of her stomach at the suggestion of a real job, especially one working with horses. "Grady said that?"

"Absolutely, and my husband does not toss compliments around lightly when it comes to his horses," Karen said. "He'd hire you in a heartbeat."

Lauren waved off the suggestion. "I don't need your money. I just need to feel as if I'm making a contribution."

"You would be," Karen insisted.

"Sounds like an ideal situation to me," Emma chimed in. "I could draw up a contract."

She was already reaching for her ever-present legal pad, when Karen scowled at her. "Put that away. We don't need a contract."

"Of course not," Lauren said. "Besides, this will

be a trial run. If it doesn't work out, it's nobody's loss.''

"I just thought if it was spelled out in black and white, everybody would understand what was expected," Emma said defensively. Drawing scowls, she reluctantly put away the pad of paper.

"That's because you think like the lawyer you are. Lauren understands, right?" Karen asked.

"Perfectly. I work with the horses in return for room and board. Sounds fair to me.''

Karen's eyes lit up. "Then it's a deal?"

Lauren gave the matter another moment of consideration, then nodded. This was precisely the reason she'd been hesitating over that new movie deal her agent had brought to her. She'd known in the pit of her stomach that something better was just around the corner.

"It's a deal," she told Karen. "I'll be back as soon as I clear up some loose ends in Los Angeles. But I won't hang out here forever. Tell Grady that the minute we decide if it's working out, I'll find my own place. I don't want him to panic that I'm settling in forever.''

Before the words were out of her mouth, she was surrounded by her friends, all of them talking at once. Now that the decision had been made, for the first time in years Lauren felt she was exactly where she was supposed to be, doing exactly what she was meant to do.

Wade Owens took one look at the woman slipping through the corral fence and felt his heart slam to a stop. He told himself it wasn't her perfect derriere that caused the reaction. Nor was it the auburn hair, caught up in a careless ponytail and gleaming like fire in the sunlight. It was the fact that she was creeping up on a stallion who didn't take kindly to strangers. What was obviously a little adventure for this tenderfoot was destined for a very bad ending.

Wade bolted toward the corral, then slowed his approach so he wouldn't be the one responsible for spooking the horse. Midnight was already shifting nervously, his eyes rolling as the woman edged closer.

Wade could hear her murmuring to the anxious stallion and, though he couldn't hear the words, her tone was low and soothing, not unlike the one he would have used. He found that tone reassuring, but he still intended to take a strip off this woman's hide for venturing into the corral in the first place. Assuming she got out in one piece, which was still a dicey prospect.

Where the hell were Grady and Karen? Why had they allowed this woman to roam around on her own? Maybe they didn't even know she was here. That had to be it. They knew how fractious Midnight was. If they were around, she would never be in harm's way.

Midnight's massive muscles rippled as she gently placed a hand on his neck. He pawed the ground, but he didn't bolt as Wade had anticipated. Those quiet murmurs continued as she reached into her pocket and drew out a cube of sugar, then held it out in the center of her palm. Midnight sniffed, then daintily took the sugar as if he'd never even once considered trampling the woman beside him.

Wade finally felt his tension ease. She obviously knew the way to Midnight's heart. The horse would lash out with deadly hooves at any prospective rider who came within ten yards of him, but he was a sucker for a treat—sugar, apples, carrots, it didn't matter. He was already nosing her pocket for more.

Her laugh was a surprise, light and joyous, as the horse nudged her none too gently, almost landing her on her very attractive backside.

"Oh no you don't. No more today," she told him, rubbing his neck.

Wade was suddenly filled with the oddest yearning to trade places with Midnight. He wondered what those slender hands would feel like caressing his skin, sliding up his chest. As the image settled in, he muttered a curse. It was a pitiful thing when a man was jealous of a horse.

After a few more minutes, the woman finally eased away from Midnight and crawled back through the fence, an expression of satisfaction on her face. It lasted until she caught sight of Wade removing his hat. He was pretty sure his scowl would have intimidated Wyatt Earp himself. He meant it to make this woman quake in her very expensive boots.

"Hi," she said, her smile coming easily—and fading just as quickly when it wasn't returned.

"What exactly did you think you were doing?" he demanded, scowl firmly in place.

Whatever uncertainty she momentarily had been feeling vanished. Wade could practically see her temper stirring to life, turning her eyes to the color of a turbulent sea.

She met his gaze without flinching. "What did it look like, cowboy?"

The only way to deal with a woman who had more sass than sense was to lay it all on the line in plain English. "It looked an awful lot like you were trying to get yourself killed and ruin a fine stallion in the process," he said with barely contained fury. "The next time you decide you want to have a chat with the stock around here, get permission. This isn't a damn riding stable, and these horses aren't pets.''

If his goal had been to intimidate her, he'd failed miserably. He saw that in a heartbeat. In fact, she took a deliberate step toward him, then another, until she was standing toe-to-toe, hands on hips, her flowery scent coming off of her in tantalizing waves. She seemed oblivious to the fact that she was barely chin-high to him. Wade swallowed hard and had to force himself not to back off. No pint-sized squirt was going to turn the tables on him, especially not when they both knew he was right.

''Now you listen to me,'' she said, poking a perfectly manicured finger into his chest. ''I was in that corral because Grady and Karen asked me to take a look at Midnight. Last I heard, this was their ranch. Is that permission good enough for you, cowboy?''

Wade regarded her skeptically. ''They asked you to go in there with that stallion? Into the corral with him? Why would they do a thing like that?''

''Maybe because I've known my way around horses since I was knee-high to a grasshopper. Maybe because—unlike *some* people—I don't try to bully them into things they're not ready to try. Maybe because gaining the trust of a horse that's been mistreated the way this one has been is something the wrangler they hired doesn't know diddly about.'' She smiled, the effect dazzling despite the phony sentiment behind it. ''That would be you, I assume.''

To Wade's everlasting regret, it was. But he was not about to get into a name-calling game with this little slip of a female. He *did* intend to have a long talk with Grady Blackhawk about just exactly who was in charge of the horses at this ranch. Last he'd heard, that was the job *he'd* been hired to do.

He leveled a look straight into those devastating blue-green eyes of hers. "Until Grady tells me otherwise, nobody goes near Midnight unless I say so. If I catch you in there again, you won't be happy about the way I get you out."

"Is that so?" she said, obviously unimpressed.

Wade slammed his hat back on his head and glowered. "Try me."

He wasn't entirely sure, but as she whirled around and walked away it almost sounded as if she murmured something along the lines of "Maybe I will."

Maybe he was crazy, maybe he was overly optimistic, but he had a feeling that she was no longer talking exclusively about continuing their test of wills over the horse. In fact, he got the distinct impression that she had something else altogether in mind. And his body responded with a slam of lust so powerful he knew he'd be a long time getting to sleep that night.

Lauren made it back to the ranch house with her spine rigid and her shoulders straight, but she was seething inside. Of all the unmitigated nerve! That man had made it sound as if she was some sort of incompetent tenderfoot. She slammed the back door behind her, went to the sink and splashed a handful of cold water on her flaming face. She jerked up when she heard a chuckle.

"I see you've met Wade Owens," Karen said, making no attempt at all to hide her amusement.

"Is that who that was?" Lauren asked. "Is he important around here or can I kill him?"

"Oh, I'd hold off for a while, if I were you. The

man knows his horses. In fact, you two have a lot in common.''

"I doubt that," Lauren said. "Arrogance and audacity are traits I try to avoid."

Karen chuckled again, her eyes alight with merriment. "Not entirely successfully, if you don't mind me saying so. I suspect you gave as good as you got out there."

Lauren frowned at her, but didn't argue. Unfortunately, few people on earth knew her better than Karen did. It would be pointless for Lauren to try to pretend with her that she was without flaws. And she had given this Wade Owens a few things to think about before she'd left him standing in the dust. Karen was right about that.

"This is better than watching one of those romantic comedies you star in," Karen added, sounding as if she had enjoyed the entire scene just a little too much. "You're all flustered and indignant. Wade's clearly in an uproar. From what I could see from here, he said more in the last ten minutes than I've heard him say over an entire meal."

"Are you saying that man is the strong, silent type?" Lauren asked incredulously, thinking of the barrage of disdainful words he'd hurled at her.

"Has been so far," Karen confirmed. "Apparently you got under his skin."

"Only because I dared to win over one of his precious horses. Apparently his ego couldn't take it."

"It was good to see you haven't lost your touch," Karen said. "Not with horses, anyway. I'm not so sure about men, though. You usually do better at charming them."

"I don't need to charm this Wade person." Why

waste her breath on a man that pigheaded? Her gaze narrowed. "Or do I? Are you telling me we have to work together?"

"It makes sense. He *is* the wrangler. Grady says he's good. What I find fascinating, though, is that your instinctive charm failed you," Karen said. "You allowed him to throw you completely off-kilter."

"I most certainly did not," Lauren argued, though she had to admit that for several minutes out there her blood had stirred in a very disconcerting way. She had liked letting her temper flare wildly out of control.

For the past ten years, she had kept a lid on it just to avoid being stereotyped as one of Hollywood's temperamental prima donnas. She had fallen into an uncharacteristic passivity in her marriages as well. Neither man had been worth getting stirred up over, which was pretty much proof that the relationships had been doomed from the start. She sighed heavily, Wade Owens forgotten for the moment.

"Why the sigh?" Karen asked.

"Just thinking of how much of my life I've wasted not being true to myself."

"You haven't wasted your life," Karen scolded. "You've accomplished what some actresses can only dream of."

"But I never wanted to be an actress. I wanted to live in Los Angeles because it was glamorous and exciting, but I would have been perfectly content to be a bookkeeper at one of the Hollywood studios. If that producer hadn't asked me to audition for his movie while we were going over his film budget, I would still be a bookkeeper. It's like the past ten years happened to some other person."

"Are you regretting the money and the fame?"

Lauren considered the question. "I don't regret them, no. How could I? It's been an incredible ride, and I know how lucky I am, but something's missing. It has been for a long time. That's why I'm back here, to see if I can find it."

It was the first time she'd made the admission aloud. To her relief, Karen didn't laugh. In fact, she seemed to be giving careful thought to Lauren's statement.

"Love?" Karen suggested. "Is that what you're searching for?"

"Could be," Lauren admitted. She had been envious watching all of her friends fall madly in love, one by one.

"Kids?"

She hadn't really thought about having a family, but, yes, that was part of it, too. She wanted to hold her own babies in her arms, buy the girls sweet little dresses and the boys shiny new trucks and decorate a nursery. Until this second, she hadn't realized just how loudly her biological clock had been ticking.

Rather than admit to all that, she said, "Or maybe I'm just looking for a healthy dose of reality. Good friends. Hard physical work. A beautiful sunset." She shrugged. "I wish I could put my finger on it."

"Maybe a man like Wade Owens could help you figure all that out," Karen suggested.

Lauren considered the square-jawed cowboy with the cold-as-flint eyes and downturned mouth. Okay, so he had broad shoulders, narrow hips and enviable muscles. So what? She gave her friend a scathing look. "First he'd have to get over himself."

Karen laughed. "Hey, I saw that little scene out there. He'd probably say the same about you." Her expression sobered. "Did you introduce yourself, by the way? Or did he recognize you?"

Lauren realized with a sense of shock that Wade hadn't seemed the least bit concerned with who she was. In fact, she was almost a hundred percent certain he'd had no idea she was anything other than an unwanted interloper. That pleased her more than she could say.

"If he did, he didn't care," she told Karen. "He was just mad as spit that I was on his turf."

"Maybe you should keep it that way," Karen said thoughtfully. "Let him get to know you without all the Hollywood glitter as a distraction. It can't be easy to find a man who can see past the image. Wouldn't that be a relief, for a change?"

"That's certainly true," Lauren agreed, seeing the benefit of clinging to a little anonymity for as long as she could. "But I'm sticking around town so I can find *myself,* not so I can find a man."

"Any reason you can't do both?"

"Maybe not, but I don't think your friend Wade would want to be considered as a candidate," she said, though she couldn't explain the vague sense of disappointment that crept over her as she said it. Why should she give two figs whether an arrogant, full-of-himself wrangler gave her a second look or not?

She forced herself to be honest. Maybe it was because he was the sexiest male she'd come across in ten long years. Maybe it was because he was so damn gritty and real that he made all the polished, sophisticated men she knew pale by comparison.

Or maybe it was just because for the first time in forever, she'd felt completely alive, with her temper close to boiling and her heart slamming in her chest.

In the last half hour she'd discovered that everything she'd experienced in recent years was little more than a two-bit imitation.

She had hoped that living in Winding River would bring her a certain amount of peace. Thanks to Karen and Grady's wrangler, she'd just discovered that it was promising to be downright fun.

Chapter Two

Wade spent the rest of the afternoon seething over his run-in with the Blackhawks' houseguest. The woman had more audacity and arrogance than any female he'd encountered in years. While that might have been stimulating in the short term, it was nothing to tangle with over the long haul.

Not that Wade was a long-haul kind of guy. He'd learned that from his daddy, God rest his sorry butt.

Blake Travis had been one of the wealthiest men in Montana when he'd met Wade's mama at the Lucky Horseshoe Saloon in Billings thirty years ago. To a woman like Arlene Owens, he had seemed like the answer to a prayer. She had fallen for him like a ton of bricks. To hear her tell it, the man had been God's gift to womankind—not just rich and powerful, but also kind and generous. He'd certainly left her with something to remember…Wade.

Unfortunately, it turned out that old Blake had a nasty habit of seeking out vulnerable women, impregnating and then abandoning them. He seemed to think it was his right to take whatever he pleased and damn the consequences. He simply bought off anyone who raised a fuss. Arlene had learned all this long after it was too late to help her protect herself.

Totally naive about his reputation, Arlene had been convinced that the man would provide for her and her baby, if only he knew about their situation. Off she'd gone to the Travis ranch outside of town to share the good news. There she'd been greeted by Blake's wife and introduced to his two legitimate sons and heirs. The long-suffering Mrs. Travis had given Arlene a modest check and assured her that it was the best she could hope for in terms of support from that sneaky, lying snake of a philanderer Blake Travis. Stunned and humiliated by the mere existence of a wife, Arlene had taken her at her word.

She had considered packing up everything she owned and moving, but a stubborn streak that Wade had inherited kept her right where she was. And once Wade was old enough to ask about his daddy, she had told him the unvarnished truth.

Over the years, Wade had built up a healthy loathing for the rich, who thought they could play havoc with people's lives and leave others to clean up their messes. His occasional chance encounters with his half-siblings had been tense affairs. He'd bloodied their noses and threatened to do worse. They'd been sent off to boarding school soon afterward, and his mother had gotten a stern warning from the sheriff that Wade was on thin ice.

When Wade turned eighteen, he'd gone to tell his

daddy just exactly what he thought of him, but Blake had had the misfortune to die before Wade could share his opinion. That had left him with a lot of outrage and no satisfactory way to rid himself of it.

It had also left him grimly determined never to find himself in the same fix. He was responsible when it came to women. He never lied. He never cheated. And he used fail-proof protection—or at least he assured himself that it was as close to fail-proof as a man could get. There would be no trail of heartbroken women or abandoned children in his life.

If and when he ever settled down, it would be for life, and with some sweet, down-to-earth woman who'd stick close to home, raise his children and never give him a moment's grief. Karen Blackhawk's friend had grief written all over her.

He muttered yet another curse at the memory of the way she'd come after him with every bit as much temper as he'd used in trying to scare the daylights out of her. With her fancy boots, designer jeans and those soft, neatly manicured hands, everything about her spoke of money. Maybe she knew horses, but he suspected whatever she'd learned had been during a childhood of privilege. If she'd ever done a hard day's work in her life, he'd eat his hat.

"Problem?" Grady asked, appearing in the stable office just as Wade uttered another colorful profanity.

"Tell that woman to stay the hell away from my horses," Wade said without a moment's thought to censoring himself with the man who'd only been his boss for a few weeks now.

Grady's lips twitched with amusement. "Had a run-in with Lauren, did you?"

"Is that her name?" He scowled at Grady, who was

still fighting a grin. "It's not funny. She's going to get herself killed. She doesn't have the sense God gave a gnat. You should have seen her. She walked right into the corral with Midnight, like he was some docile pet pony."

"So?"

"You know what that horse is capable of doing. I shudder to think about what could have happened."

"But nothing did happen, did it?" Grady said. "Wade, Lauren's no tenderfoot. She grew up around here. Karen says she learned to ride practically before she could walk. I've watched her in action."

"Oh, I can imagine that," Wade said with biting sarcasm. "She *is* something to look at, no question about that."

Grady frowned at him. "I'm talking about her skills. She's every bit as good with horses as you are," he insisted. "Give her a chance."

The praise made Wade's stomach turn over. Filled with trepidation, he studied Grady's solemn expression, then heaved a sigh. "Dammit Grady, is that an order? Please tell me you didn't go and hire her."

"Without talking to you? Of course not," Grady said, though he looked vaguely guilty when he said it.

"Then what the hell was she doing out there?"

"Like I said, she's good with horses. She's also one of Karen's best friends. She needs something to keep her occupied while she's here. We asked her to help out with the training, work with Midnight and a couple of the others that aren't doing well with the usual techniques. She'll answer to you. I'll make that clear to her. Your job is safe."

"I'm not worried about my job," Wade snapped. "I'm worried about her pretty little neck. The woman's got more guts than sense. Midnight could have squashed her like a bug. You know how he is."

"I went over his history with Lauren before she went out there. She's worked with abused animals before. She knew what she was doing," Grady insisted in yet another futile attempt to soothe Wade.

"Couldn't prove it by me," Wade retorted, still seething over the scene he'd walked up on.

"She got out of there in one piece, didn't she?" Grady reminded him, his tone mild. "Midnight didn't come to any harm, right?"

"This time," Wade conceded. "Next time, she might not be so lucky. A horse won't give a hang that she's beautiful or has a gentle touch. If he's of a mind to, he'll still kick her from here to next week, or break his own leg going wild in his stall."

Grady still didn't seem to be taking Wade's concerns all that seriously. If anything, his amusement seemed to be growing. "I'm pretty sure I heard a compliment in there somewhere. Lauren got to you, didn't she? What's really bugging you? Is it that she has a way with horses or that she looks great in a pair of jeans?"

Wade wanted to protest that it was neither, but clearly, Grady had already drawn his own conclusions. Anything Wade had to say would only add fuel to the fire. Too much protesting would have a contradictory effect.

Besides, there was some truth to what Grady said. Once he'd calmed down, Wade had been forced to admit that he admired Lauren's refusal to back down from either Midnight or from him. And her tush did do amazing things for a pair of faded jeans. There was no denying that, so why bother trying?

"Are you telling me to let her do whatever strikes

her fancy where the horses are concerned?'' he asked Grady, unable to keep a note of resignation from his voice. He wanted to be very clear on his boss's expectations and where to place the responsibility for any disasters that took place.

"As long as it's not going to get her killed, yes,'' Grady said.

Wade shrugged, aware that any further argument would be a waste of breath. Until something disastrous happened, he'd go along with it, as long as Grady understood that any calamity was on his head. "Okay, then,'' he told him. "It's your ranch and your insurance.''

"And your reputation,'' Grady pointed out, his expression just a little too doggone innocent to suit Wade.

"How's that?'' Wade asked, his gaze narrowed.

"Everybody knows you're in charge of the horses around here. It's your reputation that will suffer if you let anything happen to Lauren on your watch.''

Well, hell. His boss had just set a pretty tidy little trap for him.

"I had a talk with Wade this evening,'' Grady said as he joined Karen and Lauren around the dinner table.

Lauren's gaze shot up. "Oh?'' She could just imagine what kind of remarks Wade would have made about their encounter. Still, Grady didn't look overly upset, so maybe the man had been smart enough to keep his opinions to himself.

"He understands that you're going to be helping with the horses,'' Grady added.

"How does he feel about that?'' she asked. Not that it mattered to her, but it might to Grady.

Grady grinned. "Pretty much like you'd expect after

the run-in you two had. He has some reservations, but he's withholding judgment for the time being.''

''How noble of him,'' Lauren snapped, and shoved aside her plate. ''Maybe this isn't such a good idea, after all. You're paying him good money to handle your stock. I'm sure he's very good at his job. I don't want to create problems by getting in his way. None of us really knows if I'm going to make a worthwhile contribution around here. Maybe it's best if I bow out and leave it to the experts.''

Karen shot a warning gaze at her husband. ''Lauren, you're not the problem. And if Wade has a problem, he'll get over it. We want you here—right, Grady?''

''Of course,'' he said at once, surreptitiously reaching below the table to rub his shin, which Karen had apparently kicked. ''From what I heard, you managed to get in that corral with Midnight. Nobody else has been able to get near him, not even Wade.''

Lauren's spirits brightened. ''Really?''

''That horse kicks up a fuss like you wouldn't believe when Wade gets anywhere close,'' Grady confirmed. ''Knowing his history, I probably shouldn't have agreed to buy Midnight, but I couldn't bear the thought of him being put down because no one could handle him. It's not the horse's fault that his last owner was a mean son of a bitch.''

''You're right,'' Lauren said. ''He's a spectacular animal. It'll take time, but I guarantee he'll be worth every bit of effort I put into him.''

Grady exchanged a look with his wife, then asked Lauren, ''You're making Midnight your special mission, then?''

Lauren nodded, accepting the challenge without hesitation. Not just because she'd fallen in love with the

high-spirited creature, but because it would give Wade
Owens fits to have to sit by and watch her succeed
where he had failed.

"Because you believe in him or because you want
to show Wade up?" Grady teased.

"Does it matter?" Lauren said, refusing to admit
that he'd hit the nail on the head. "Either way, you get
what you want."

Grady chuckled. "This is going to be better entertainment than the westerns on TNT."

Lauren held up her glass of tea in a mock toast. "So
glad I'm able to provide you newlyweds with a diver-
sion."

"Oh, I can think of plenty of things to do that are
more exciting than watching you tie that man up in
knots," Karen retorted, turning a heated gaze on her
husband.

"Come to think of it, so can I," he said, kicking his
chair back as he reached for her hand and then pulled
her from the room.

"I'll do the dishes," Lauren called after them, barely
containing a laugh at the speed of their departure.

Still, after they'd gone, she sighed, unable to stop
the wave of envy that washed over her. She'd been
married twice, but she had never been in love like that,
never taken one look at her husband and forgotten
about everything else. Maybe she'd spent too many
years faking emotions on-screen to know the real thing
when it came along.

Thinking about that, she absentmindedly finished off
the leftovers, then groaned at the amount of food she
had eaten. It was more than she consumed in two days
when she was working on a movie. At this rate, unless
she exercised hard for a solid three hours every day,

she'd be as big as a house by the end of summer. Already, her size-four jeans were getting snug in the waist, and she'd barely been here twenty-four hours.

It doesn't matter.

The shocking words echoed in her head. Lauren dropped down on a chair and stared at the empty lasagna dish with a sense of astonishment. For the first time in ten years, her weight actually didn't matter. Nor did her dress size. She was finally free of all of the unnaturally rigid self-control she'd been forced to live by from the moment she'd taken up a career in front of a camera.

"Oh, my," she murmured, reaching for the last piece of garlic bread as a final act of defiance. It was loaded with butter and garlic, and it tasted absolutely heavenly, even though it was no longer warm from the oven.

A tap on the back door had her looking up guiltily and brushing crumbs from her lips.

"What's this? Pigging out on the food I brought by last night to celebrate your arrival?" Gina asked, grinning.

"I am," Lauren said, shoving aside that nagging guilt. "And you know what? I don't care."

"Uh-oh, is there a rebellion in the making?"

"There is," Lauren confirmed. She eyed the box in Gina's hand eagerly. "Did you bring dessert?"

"Cheesecake, as a matter of fact. I was experimenting with a tiramisu flavor. Rafe had to fly to New York this morning, so I'm looking for a guinea pig."

"You've found one," Lauren said enthusiastically, getting up to grab plates from the cupboard.

"Where are Grady and Karen?" Gina asked.

Lauren directed a pointed look toward the ceiling.

Gina grinned. "Ah, newlyweds. I keep forgetting that they're never available after dinnertime. I'm glad Rafe and I aren't like that."

Lauren hooted. "Only because he's still out of town so much. Just wait till he moves his practice out here and hooks up with Emma. She's so efficient, she'll have them both out the door every afternoon by four. You'll be just as disgusting as Grady and Karen."

"Jealous?" Gina asked.

Though the question was meant to be teasing, Lauren considered it seriously. "You know, I am."

"Then we definitely have to get busy and find you a man. After all, you were the one who was matchmaking like a crazy woman all during the reunion. You practically threw me at Rafe."

"Of course, that was before we knew he'd followed you out here in the first place to try to put you in jail," Lauren said.

"Actually, he wanted to put my business partner in jail. I was just a means to an end." Gina grinned. "Then there was Emma. Weren't you the one who pushed her into Ford's arms at the dance?"

"No, that was our English teacher. I actually tried to set her up with some guy who turned out to be an exterminator from Des Moines who's married to one of our old classmates. It was not one of my shining moments."

"Still, turnabout is fair play," Gina insisted. "There must be someone around who's worthy of you."

Lauren thought of her reaction to Wade Owens earlier in the day. Instant animosity was probably not what Gina had in mind, but there had been a lot of electricity crackling in the air this afternoon. It was just as well that her friend didn't know about her encounter with the sexy wrangler.

She took a deliberate bite of cheesecake, savoring the smooth texture and fabulous flavor. "Oh, sweet heaven," she murmured. "Who needs men when there's cheesecake like this? It's sinful."

Gina beamed. "Yes, but this pleasure is short-lived. A man's forever."

"If you're lucky," Lauren said. "I've had two who barely lasted till the ink was dry on the wedding license."

"Oh, don't be so cynical," Gina said with a dismissive wave of her hand. "They were jerks. We're talking about a real man."

Once again, an image of Wade popped into Lauren's head. With that whipcord-lean body he was a real man, no doubt about that.

"What?" Gina said, staring at her curiously. "You've already met someone, haven't you?"

"Don't be ridiculous. I've only been here a couple of days. I've barely left the house. Why would you think that?"

"Because of your expression."

"My expression? What about it?"

"It went all dreamy there for a minute. You can't fake a look like that, and only one thing can cause it— a man. Who is he?"

"You're crazy," Lauren insisted. "And if you keep bugging me, I'm going to tell everybody in town that your cheesecake tastes like spoiled cottage cheese and has the texture of sand."

Gina regarded her with a horrified expression. "You wouldn't dare."

"Try me." Even as she uttered the words, Lauren

recalled that same dare coming from Wade's lips earlier in the day. And what had she said? *Maybe I will.* Those were certainly words meant to get a man all riled up. What had she been thinking?

"Why do I have the feeling you're having some sort of flashback?" Gina asked, studying her intently. "It's that man again, isn't it?"

"I'm telling you, there is no man."

Gina patted her hand. "Keep telling *yourself* that. I spent a lot of time in denial where Rafe was concerned, too. So did Emma with Ford, and Karen with Grady, and Cassie with Cole. Just look at us now. I recognize the signs."

Lauren shuddered. Gina couldn't be right. Her with Wade Owens? She wouldn't allow it.

Then again, if her friends were anything to judge by, she might not actually have much say in the matter.

Chapter Three

Lauren got up at the crack of dawn, filled her pockets with treats for Midnight—apples this time—then decided she deserved a hearty breakfast herself before she went out to work with the horse and risked an encounter with Wade. Both were going to require stamina, to say nothing of all her wits.

Even though she was up early, Grady and Karen were already long gone. A still-warm pot of coffee sat on the stove, along with two fresh eggs just gathered from the henhouse and a plate of crisp bacon. Lauren would have settled for cereal or toast, but an honest-to-goodness breakfast was too tempting to pass up.

Twenty minutes later, her stomach full, she carried her cup of coffee out to the porch and sat down with a sigh of pure contentment. The sun had just broken over the horizon in the east, splashing the rolling hills of the Snowy Range with a golden wash. The last lingering patches of snow glistened at the peaks.

A dozen meditation sessions couldn't create the powerful serenity that stole through her now.

"This is the smartest thing I've ever done," she said contentedly as she sipped her coffee and planned her morning. How often had she had the luxury of taking the time to plan her own day, the freedom to do whatever struck her fancy? Lauren couldn't even remember the last time she'd had that opportunity. Too much of her life had been controlled by production schedules, publicity tours and endless rounds of meetings to discuss future film projects. Well, no more. She would be captive to nothing other than the rhythm of ranch life and her own limited role in it.

For now, the schedule would be especially light. An hour with Midnight, letting him get used to her presence and begin to accept her touch, would probably be as much as the horse could handle. After that, she'd take a drive over to Winding River, maybe try to scare up Emma and Gina to join her for lunch at Stella's. What was the point of moving back if she didn't grab every chance to be with her friends? The realization—after years of hurried phone calls and quick visits—that they would be nearby day in and day out, available for birthdays and holidays, still amazed and delighted Lauren.

The ringing of the phone snapped her out of her pleasant reverie. Habit had her running inside to grab the receiver, despite the likelihood that the call concerned ranch business.

"Blackhawk Ranch," she said.

"Lauren, is that you?"

Lauren sighed at the sound of an all-too-familiar

voice. Jason Matthews was an outstanding agent. He was an ardent champion for his clients, a real fighter. A few months ago she had loved that about him. Now that he refused to take no for an answer from her, she considered the trait less desirable.

She could envision Jason in his office, wearing a headset phone so his hands could be free to work the keys on his computer. He was probably going over his stock portfolio as they talked. For a man barely into his thirties, he was already obsessed with his retirement plan. He was always at his desk in Beverly Hills by the time Wall Street opened, on the phone to his broker ten minutes later.

"Hello, Jason. I thought when we said goodbye the other day, you understood what the word meant," she said. "Why are you calling?"

"It's taken some real hardball negotiating, but the studio just agreed to a higher figure if you'll sign for that comedy we talked about," he said, sounding exceedingly pleased with himself. "It'll make you the highest-paid woman in films after Julia Roberts."

Her heart sank. They'd already had this discussion— several times in fact. "Jason, I'm having a flashback here. Didn't you call me a few days ago when I was packing my bags and say almost exactly the same words?"

"This is a new offer, even more money, and a percentage of the gross. They want you, Lauren, and they want you bad." He was triumphant.

"Lovely, but my answer's still the same," she said. "I'm not interested in doing this project or any other project. Why are you still negotiating?"

"Because that's what I do," he explained patiently. "It's what you pay me the big bucks to do. I want you to get every penny you're worth. You're the second-biggest female box-office star in the country these days. This film will set the precedent for every deal you do from here on out. It's important to get it right."

Lauren sighed. "But, Jason, you're missing the point. I'm not going to do this film, period."

"Of course you are."

"I am not, so stop trying to run the money up. You're wasting your time and theirs. How's it going to look when they discover that I never intended to commit? You're going to end up with a lot of egg on your handsome little face. Your credibility will be shot when you can't deliver me."

Her response was met by a long silence. "I don't get it," he said finally, clearly bemused by her attitude. In Jason's world no one turned down the kind of money the studio had just put on the table. No one quit at the height of success, unless it was part of some publicity gambit to up the stakes.

"Is it the script?" he asked. "We talked about that. They'll bring in a new writer to tweak it. You can have anybody you want."

"The script is fabulous the way it is," Lauren assured him. "I'm just not interested. How many times do I have to say that?"

"Until you make a believer out of me," he retorted, evidently still unconvinced. "Whoops, hold on a sec. Ken just stuck a note under my nose. The studio's on the other line."

He sounded so gleeful. Clearly he hadn't heard one word she'd said. "I am not holding on," she told him, seizing the excuse to end the frustrating call. "I have to go."

"Why? What's more important than this?" Jason demanded.

"I have a date with a horse," she said, and hung up before he could respond.

Because she knew Jason would call back a half-dozen times or more before he gave up for the day—and then only so she could sleep on the latest offer and he could begin the badgering again fresh in the morning—she left the house at once and headed for the corral. If there was any more communicating to be done, Jason could do it with the answering machine. He obviously didn't care about much besides the sound of his own voice anyway.

Across the yard, the corral was empty, but as Lauren moved toward the open pasture beyond, she spotted Midnight. She climbed onto the split-rail fence and watched him. His black coat glistening in the sun, he was all alone, far from the other horses who'd been turned out that morning. After a moment, his proud head rose. He sniffed the air and his ears twitched. Slowly he turned in her direction, and it was as if he was studying her with the same intensity she had been directing his way.

Lauren took a piece of apple from her pocket and held it out. Midnight whinnied and shook his head, as if he was declining the tempting offer, but a minute later the powerful stallion with the blaze of white on his face trotted sedately toward her. He stopped a few feet away, still cautious.

"If you want this, you're going to have to come and get it," Lauren said quietly, still holding the apple out toward him.

Midnight pranced away.

"Okay, then." She started to put the fruit back in

her pocket, but a whinny of protest made her pause. She bit back a smile. "Think it over. I can wait."

She sat there patiently, perfectly still, the sweet chunk of apple in plain sight. With something that sounded almost like a sigh, Midnight edged closer until he could take it daintily from her hand. Satisfied with the treat and the lack of danger from the human who'd offered it, he came closer still and nuzzled at her pocket. Only then did Lauren dare to touch him.

She rubbed her hand along his sleek neck. Though he didn't skittishly dance away, he trembled at her light touch. The reaction was telling. The knowledge that someone had badly mistreated this magnificent animal made Lauren sick to her stomach. But the fact that he was already beginning to trust her humbled her.

"Good morning, handsome," she murmured.

"You talking to me?" a low-pitched masculine voice inquired lazily.

Lauren's head snapped around to find Wade standing just inches behind her, close enough to send Midnight dancing away. She watched the horse leave with real regret, then turned back to the man.

How had she missed Wade's approach or the heat radiating from his body? Once again she was struck by the way he managed to make an ordinary T-shirt and jeans look like designer clothing. No man had a right to look that good, that tempting, at this hour of the morning.

Better yet, he was holding two mugs of steaming coffee. He offered her one.

"I saw you heading over this way and decided this would be a good time to make peace," he explained.

She accepted the cup with caution. "Then the coffee's not laced with arsenic?"

"Not by me," he assured her. "You got any enemies around I don't know about?"

"Not in Winding River," she said, leaving out the fact that there were quite a few people in Hollywood who wouldn't shed any tears if she disappeared forever. She'd discovered that jealousy and greed could turn friend to enemy overnight in the film business. Actresses she'd considered friends had bailed when she won a coveted role. Award nominations stirred envy, but that was almost the least of it. Everything had been a competition, with winners and losers.

Glad to be away from all that, she took an appreciative sip of the coffee. "Thanks. I needed this." The talk with her agent had used up all Lauren's reserves of energy.

"Not usually up this early?" Wade asked, the disdain back in his voice.

She sighed. For a minute there she'd almost believed they could make a fresh start. Instead, it had apparently been a lull before a new barrage of insults.

"Always up this early," she corrected, determined not to escalate the fight. Let Wade do that, if he couldn't stop himself. "But I'll never get used to it. I'm a night owl by nature."

"Hard to be a night owl on a ranch. Too many chores have to be done at daybreak."

"And I grew up doing most of them," she said. "I might not like morning, but I follow through on my responsibilities."

He seemed duly chastised by the rebuke. "Look, Miss…"

"Lauren will do."

He nodded. "Okay, then, Lauren. We obviously got off on the wrong foot yesterday. And it sounds as if we're pretty darn close to doing the same thing again. How about if we start fresh with no preconceived notions? I'm Wade, by the way.''

Given the fact that he wasn't going to go away, Lauren was more than willing to meet him halfway. They were going to have to work together. It made more sense to be friends than enemies. She held out her hand. ''Nice to meet you, Wade.''

He took her outstretched hand in a grasp that was warm and all-too-brief. Even that quick brush of callused fingers across softer skin was enough to send a jolt of awareness through her. Work-roughened hands had always been more appealing to her than the manicured hands of most of her male costars. Hands with the texture of sandpaper could bring the skin alive. Just the thought was enough to make her tremble the way Midnight had earlier.

Wade studied her with a knowing look. ''Cold?''

''No. I'm fine,'' she said, embarrassed at having been caught reacting to his touch. ''So, what's the plan? I assume you have one.''

''Grady says I should let you try whatever you like with the horses, as long as you don't get yourself killed. Since that's not a notion that's real popular with me either, how about going for a ride with me? Let me see how you handle yourself on a horse. Maybe I'll be more reassured than I was yesterday.''

She chafed at the test, but she understood it. If she were in his position, she'd do the same thing. And since it was clear that Grady had tried to smooth things over, she owed it to him to give Wade at least a passing show of respect.

Still, she couldn't resist a taunt. ''Shall I take Midnight?'' she inquired innocently.

He regarded her soberly, his gray eyes cool and assessing. "Only if you don't care about coming back," he said, not giving away by so much as a blink whether he was serious.

"Then I'll save him for next time," she said. "Since you know the animals better than I do, you choose one today. And don't go with the slowest nag in the barn, or I'll make you regret it."

"How about we compromise?" he suggested, though it looked as if the word stuck in his craw.

"Now there's a novel idea. I'm surprised you're familiar with the concept."

To her surprise, he winked at her. "Oh, you'd be amazed at the things I'll do given the right incentive."

She laughed. "That must mean Grady's offered you a huge bonus for putting up with me."

"Not a dime," he insisted. "But he did lead me to believe that you weren't a tenderfoot and that I owed it to you and the ranch to give you a fair chance."

"Okay, then, what's the compromise?"

"You pick your own horse, subject to my okay."

Lauren nodded. "Fair enough." She'd ridden almost every horse in the Blackhawk barn at one time or another.

A half hour later, they'd saddled up. Once Wade had explained that they might as well ride up into the hills to see if they could locate some wild horses that had been reported, Lauren abandoned her plan to go into town. Instead, she took the time to pack a couple of thick ham-and-cheese sandwiches and some of Gina's extraordinary cheesecake along with a thermos of iced tea. If Wade thought he was going to put her through her paces, she was at least going to be well fortified for the experience.

"Maybe, if you're as good as Grady says, you can talk those mustangs into coming back with us," he taunted when she returned from the kitchen with their lunch. "I'm always looking for new stock at a good price. Can't beat free."

"Very amusing. I think Grady may have oversold my skill, if he has you believing I'm capable of sweet-talking a few wild stallions down into the corral."

Wade's gaze traveled over her from head to foot in an assessment deliberately meant to rile her. "You could always practice on me, see if you can tame me."

Lauren's heart thumped erratically at the suggestion. "Something tells me that you're tougher than any horse I might tangle with."

"Probably so, which is part of the challenge," he agreed, then grinned as he shoved a battered Stetson on his head. "Let's ride."

He set off at a sedate pace that Lauren had no difficulty at all matching, but the instant they hit an open stretch of land, he urged his horse to a full gallop. As if that were going to intimidate her, she thought with amusement as she urged her horse ahead of his.

His grin spread. "So that's the way it's going to be," he shouted, shooting past her.

The rush of the wind, the exhilaration of the challenge, the taunting of an infuriating man—all of it made Lauren almost giddy with pure delight. She felt vibrantly alive for the first time in months. No, in years.

Riding had always been that way for her, but this was even more so. Having Wade's gaze on her, watching as doubt turned to respect, seeing an unwilling flare of heat replace the chilly disdain that he'd expressed in more ways than one, it reminded her of the first day she'd walked onto a movie set.

Everyone from the director to the cameraman and the grips had assumed that she was yet another of the producer's whims. Heck, even she hadn't been convinced that she had any right to be on that soundstage with an Oscar-winning actor and a woman whose every film had been a critical success, if not a box-office blockbuster.

But Lauren had taken the job seriously. She had her lines down cold, and ignoring the festival the butterflies were having in her stomach, she went to work. She had played that tiny scene with every bit of emotion and passion that she could call upon.

At the end of the take, the soundstage had been dead silent for a full minute before applause had erupted. Never before—or since—had any applause been as sweet. That her first performance had been recognized with an Academy Award nomination had been the icing on the cake for Lauren. Never had any success felt as hard-won.

Until today—right here, right now—with Wade Owens slowly beginning to relax, with the judgment in his eyes easing and fire replacing ice as his gaze met hers. He drew back on the reins, and his horse slowed.

"Ready for some lunch?" he asked as casually as if the last two hours had been no more than a friendly ride in the park.

So, Lauren thought, he wasn't going to offer even token praise. That was okay. She knew he'd been impressed. He didn't have to say the words, not today. One of these days, though, she would manage to coax him into giving her her due.

"I'm starved," she admitted, dismounting.

Once she'd seen that the horse was cooled down and

had water, she joined Wade under the shade of a cottonwood tree.

"Where'd you learn to ride like that?" he asked as he gratefully accepted one of the sandwiches she'd brought along.

"My father insisted I learn practically before I could walk," she told him. "We didn't have a lot of help around our ranch, so when I got a little older, he also insisted that I do my share. That meant I had to be as good as the men so I could pull my own weight."

"How old were you when you were expected to do the same chores as everybody else?"

"I started helping when I was about eight, I guess. It took a little longer before my dad was satisfied that I wasn't slacking off."

Wade regarded her with sympathy. "Your father sounds like a hard man."

Lauren had never really thought of him that way. He was just a man trying to eke out a living for his family and everyone was expected to do their part. Her older brother, Joe, had had it tougher than she had—so tough that he'd left home at sixteen and never returned. She had idolized him, and she'd been devastated when he left without a word. At some point, though, she had been forced to conclude that his love for her hadn't been nearly as deep as hers had been for him. Even now, after all this time, she had no idea if Joe was dead or alive. She feared he was dead, because he hadn't come out of the woodwork to ask for a handout once her face had been plastered all over magazines and tabloids.

"My father had a hard life, but he wasn't a hard man," she said slowly. "I can't explain it. I thrived on the challenge, and I always had the feeling that he

never asked more of me than he thought I could
achieve. There's a lot to be said for growing up like
that. I've never been afraid of hard work and I've always believed I could do anything I set my mind to.''

"Yet, you left,'' Wade pointed out. "At least that's
the impression I got from Grady, that you'd been away
for a while.''

Lauren stiffened. Karen had been right. As long as
Wade hadn't recognized her, she wanted to cling to her
anonymity a little longer. It was nice to be with a man
who might be interested in the woman, not the image.

"I was away for several years,'' she told him.

"Where'd you go?''

"Los Angeles,'' she said cautiously, watching his
face closely. Mentioning the city didn't seem to trigger
any sort of connection between her and films.

"That's about as far removed from Winding River,
Wyoming, as a person can get,'' he said. "Why
there?''

"It seemed like it would be exciting,'' she said. That
much was true. While she had never resented the work
her father had piled on, back then it hadn't been what
she wanted. And once her beloved brother had gone,
the allure of faraway places had intensified. Maybe
she'd even had the wild idea that someday she would
find Joe, talk him into coming home and making peace
with the family. She knew it was what her father
wanted, even though he'd never mentioned her
brother's name after the day he'd run off.

"Was it as exciting as you'd hoped?'' Wade asked,
studying her intently.

"It had its moments,'' she said candidly.

"Yet, you came back.''

She shrugged. "It ran out of good moments.''

"And your parents? Are they still around here? Why aren't you with them instead of the Blackhawks?"

"They've moved."

"I see. So, what's the deal? Are you planning on sticking around?"

"As long as there's something for me to do and as long as Grady and Karen will have me," she said.

His gaze narrowed. "And then what? You'll run away again?"

Lauren wished she could be sure, because there was an intensity in Wade's eyes that suggested her answer now was important in some way. "I didn't run away back then. I was looking for something."

"Which you apparently didn't find."

She nodded. "Which I *definitely* didn't find." She met his gaze. "What about you? How'd you end up in Winding River? I know you're not from around here, or I'd have remembered you."

"Oh? Why is that?" The wink of a dimple taunted her. "Am I that memorable?"

"You are, but then this is a small place. I remember everyone, especially the men who are the most annoying."

He winced. "Ouch. A direct hit."

He reached for the untouched half of her sandwich, but she moved it out of his reach. "Oh, no, at least not till I get an answer to my question."

"I seem to have forgotten it."

"How sad that a man of your tender years is losing his short-term memory," she said. "How did you end up working for Grady?"

"I was working at a ranch a couple of hundred miles from here. I didn't like the way things were going, and someone told me Grady was looking for a wrangler. We talked. I got the job.''

"Do you come and go a lot?"

That chill returned to his eyes, turning them as dark as a sky threatening snow. "What is it you really want to know, Lauren? Are you asking if I'm reliable? Grady's already interviewed me. He's satisfied with my past and my performance.''

"So he says," she agreed. "But that doesn't keep me from wanting to make sure you're not going to bolt on my friends at the worst possible time.''

"As long as things are working out, I won't bolt," he said. "Satisfied?"

"Not really. Who gets to decide if things are working out?"

"Me and Grady.''

"I notice which one of you came first.''

"How's that any different from you deciding to take off from whatever you were doing in California? Or did you get fired and come crawling back here with your tail tucked between your legs?''

"Hardly," she retorted. Unwilling to elaborate, though, she forced a smile. "And you're right. It's no different, except that in your case my friends are involved, and nobody hurts them without taking me on in the process.''

He gave an exaggerated shudder clearly meant to mock her. "I'm trembling in my boots.''

"You should be. Believe it or not, you've seen me on my best behavior. Once I get riled up, a tornado seems tame by comparison. If you doubt that, I can give you a long list of testimonials.''

His lips twitched. "Is that so?"

"Yep," she said, then rose gracefully to her feet. "If you don't believe it, just try me."

As she walked off to get her horse, she was almost certain she heard him put his own twist on her words from the day before.

"I just might do that, Miss Lauren," he murmured, but then he drew his Stetson down over his eyes and leaned back against the tree as if he didn't have another thought to spare for her.

Lauren cast one last scathing look in Wade's direction, mounted her horse and headed back to the ranch.

"It'll be a cold day in hell before that man gets a chance to try," she muttered as she rubbed down her horse, checked his feed and then stalked into the house.

For a few fleeting moments, she and Wade Owens had actually seemed to be on the road to a peaceful coexistence. It hadn't taken much to shatter that illusion, though.

Oh, well, she had dealt with her share of pigheaded men over time. It was just too darn bad that this one was sexy as sin.

Chapter Four

As soon as he heard the sound of pounding hooves, Wade lifted the Stetson shading his eyes and watched Lauren race away. The woman could ride, no doubt about that. He'd deliberately set a tough pace for her earlier, but she hadn't been the least bit fazed by it. In fact, she'd come darn close to beating him at his own game. Okay, for a few minutes there, she *had* beat him. If he hadn't been so impressed, he might have found it annoying.

More important from his perspective, there was no question that she knew how to get to Midnight. The horse was skittish as could be around him and had been from the beginning, with no evidence of improvement. But in twenty-four hours, Lauren had the stallion literally eating out of her hand. If she could accomplish a miracle with Midnight, he had no quarrel with her sticking around. He had big plans for that horse. He couldn't help wondering, though, if Lauren knew about them.

More important, he wondered if she really would be here long enough to finish the job or if this was some temporary lark. Something told him she had the same capacity for restlessness that he had. He hadn't bought that stuff about the allure of California fading. He had a hunch she was just the type who moved on whenever the mood struck her. Though they hadn't gotten into what kind of work she'd been doing out there, for all he knew she'd changed jobs once a year or even more frequently.

That was yet another reason to steer clear of her, he warned himself. Why invest any emotion in a female who wouldn't be here long enough for him to learn much more than her name…which, come to think of it, he didn't actually know. Just Lauren, she'd told him. What was that all about? Didn't she see any point in full disclosure with the hired help?

"Don't be a jerk, Wade," he muttered as he mounted his horse and headed farther up into the hills to see if he could spot the wild horses that had eluded them earlier. It wasn't as if Lauren whoever-she-was was important in the overall scheme of his life. Why should he give two hoots what sort of secrets she was keeping hidden or what kind of snob she was? As long as she did what Grady asked of her and stayed out of Wade's way, the rest didn't matter, right?

But Wade hadn't reached the age of thirty without developing at least a modicum of honesty and self-awareness. He cared—especially about that uppity streak—because the woman got to him. She'd been turning his perceptions inside out from the moment they'd met. That ability she had to take him by surprise was more intriguing than it should be. He had a hunch it could get him into trouble before all was said and done.

Which meant just one thing...for his own peace of mind, he needed to stay the hell away from her.

Lauren was dusty, hot and tired, yet surprisingly exhilarated, by the time she walked back into the house to find Karen pouring two glasses of lemonade.

"I saw you coming," Karen said, holding one of the glasses out. "Judging from the sour expression on your face, I thought you might need something cool and equally tart to drink."

Lauren ignored the comment on her apparent mood, accepted the ice-cold glass and drank thirstily. "Just what the doctor ordered."

Karen sipped her own lemonade and studied Lauren over the rim of her glass. "Good day?" she inquired eventually.

"Productive," Lauren responded.

"In what way?"

She grinned. "I beat Wade's butt in an impromptu race he set up to try to show off."

Karen chuckled. "Haven't you learned anything? Beating a man at his own game is no way to win his heart."

"I'm not going for Wade's heart."

"Oh? What are you after?"

"His respect," she said at once, surprised to find that it was true. If that morning's ride had been meant to test her, it had also shown her that Wade was as skilled a rider as she was and then some. After dealing with him the last couple of days and seeing him in action, she had a feeling he gave his respect grudgingly, and she wanted to earn it.

Karen grinned at her response. "I see. Even more fascinating."

Lauren scowled. "Why?"

"Because there's no reason to want a man's respect unless you think he's worthy of your own."

"Yes, well, that remains to be seen," Lauren said, not prepared to make that kind of admission, even to one of her best friends. "He's still too full of himself."

And yet there had been those moments—brief though they had been—when she and Wade had connected on some level. It wasn't just chemistry, she told herself. It was something more, something with potential.

"As if," she muttered.

"As if what?" Karen asked, looking intrigued.

"Nothing."

Karen chuckled, her expression knowing. "There it is again. Oh, this is going to be fun."

"What?"

"Watching you fall like a ton of bricks. I can hardly wait to tell Emma and the others. They've been placing bets lately on when your turn would come. Now that you're actually right here under their noses, they're each going to be doing everything they possibly can to be the one who sets you up with the right man. I love it that I'm already in the lead on that and they don't even know it."

Lauren frowned. "Don't be so smug. Gina suspects. She was out here after you and Grady went to bed. She picked up on some things I said and got all sorts of crazy ideas into her head."

"Oh, really? Such as?"

"Never mind. I am not playing this game. My turn has already rolled around twice—with disastrous results," Lauren reminded her. "I don't intend to go that route again."

"Oh, piddle," Karen responded. "Those men weren't worthy enough to shine your shoes. As for Wade, I think he's a man of real substance."

"And you know that how? He hasn't even been here a month."

"Sometimes you just know these things," Karen said loftily.

"Yeah, like you knew it the first time you looked into Grady's eyes," Lauren retorted. "You thought he was a thieving scoundrel."

Karen shrugged off that little reminder. "We did have a few issues to iron out, you're right, but that just made things a little livelier. And don't try to change the subject. I can hardly wait to share this good news with the rest of the Calamity Janes."

"Don't you dare," Lauren said, annoyed because she hadn't been able to convince Karen that there was no news to spread. Sweet heaven, once people started talking, it would be no time at all before the news somehow reached the tabloids, and that would be the end of her anonymity. There was always someone willing to leak gossip about a celebrity for the right price.

"Or what?" Karen taunted, much as she had when they were girls.

"I'll have a little talk with Grady," Lauren responded, deciding that a very personal threat was better than trying to explain to the uninitiated Karen about the hot market for gossip. Karen hadn't had her life dissected on the front pages of newspapers for years, but she did care what Grady thought of her. In fact, Karen was already looking a little pale.

"About?" Karen asked suspiciously.

"Oh, I'm sure there are a lot of things he doesn't know about the Calamity Janes in their prime," Lauren said blithely. "I seem to recall one particular incident in which his beloved, honorable, sedate wife was caught mooning the school principal."

"I never did that," Karen protested, her cheeks turning red. "Not intentionally anyway. I had no idea he was anywhere around."

"The point is, you did it, and I have witnesses."

"Okay, okay, I won't say a word about you and Wade."

"There is no 'me and Wade,'" Lauren reminded her.

"No, of course not," Karen said dutifully, though she couldn't quite mask the twinkle in her eyes. "I'll try to remember that when your expression goes all soft and mushy every time his name is mentioned."

"It does not," Lauren said, horrified. "Does it?"

"If you don't believe me, ask Grady."

"I am not asking Grady anything of the kind," Lauren said. "In fact, I think I'll avoid you two altogether and drive over to Winding River. Maybe I can find somebody who's actually nice to me and buy them an expensive steak dinner at Stella's."

"Not tonight you won't," Karen said, her expression smug. "It's meat-loaf night at Stella's, which means that's where Grady and I are headed as soon as he gets back. Care to join us?"

Lauren sighed. Why bother trying to fight the inevitable? "I suppose, but I'm buying."

"I'll let you and Grady fight that battle," Karen said.

"Oh, and just so you know, Wade usually turns up for Stella's meat loaf, too."

Wade had gotten into the habit of driving to Winding River for his evening meals when he first started working for Grady. Though his boss invited him to share meals at the main house, watching Grady and Karen make eyes at each other had given Wade a strange feeling. If he hadn't known better, he would have said it was envy. He'd never seen two people any crazier in love or less reticent about public displays of affection.

At any rate, he'd started by going to the Heartbreak, having a few beers and a sandwich, but the place was too smoky for his taste and the food was lousy. After a couple of nights, even the music began to grate on his nerves. All that love-gone-wrong stuff was too depressing given his own unattached state.

Now he alternated between Tony's, where he could get a decent pizza or some filling pasta, and Stella's, where the nightly special was guaranteed to remind him of the kind of meal a man's mother should have made. Of course, his never had. He'd been lucky to get a frozen dinner that had been nuked beyond recognition. Cooking hadn't been Arlene's forte, and most nights she'd been at work anyway. He'd been left to his own devices. Learning to cook had been a matter of self-preservation, but he hadn't taken to it. Now that he had decent options a few miles away, he was eating a whole lot better.

Of course, he had quickly discovered that his new routine wouldn't guarantee him much privacy. Karen and Grady had a lot of friends, and most of them turned up at one restaurant or another every night of the week, especially since Karen's pal Gina had taken over the kitchen at Tony's.

He'd also discovered that he could count on bumping into Grady and Karen themselves on meat-loaf night at Stella's. Unfortunately, the food was too good to sacrifice just so he could avoid spending time with the newlyweds.

What he hadn't expected when he'd walked through the door tonight was to find Lauren sitting in a booth with the Blackhawks. Grady promptly beckoned him over.

"Have a seat," Grady said. He seemed oblivious to the satisfied smirk on his wife's face.

Wade hesitated, his gaze on Lauren. "I don't want to intrude."

"Oh, for goodness' sakes, sit down," she grumbled ungraciously. "I'm sure we can manage to be civil for an hour or so." She turned a sour look on Karen and added, "If we can't, we'll never hear the end of it."

Wade grinned. "If it gets to be too much of a trial, I'll eat fast."

Karen chuckled, then quickly covered her grin.

"What?" Grady said, looking from his wife to Wade, and then at Lauren. "Did I miss something?"

"No, my darling man, you are as astute as ever," Lauren assured him. "Your wife's just being an annoying meddler."

Wade slid into the booth next to Lauren just as the words crossed her lips. When his thigh brushed against hers, color flamed in her cheeks and her mouth snapped shut. Satisfied with her telling reaction, he regarded her innocently. "Anything wrong?"

"Not a thing," she said, her jaw clenched tight.

He patted her hand. "Good. Now stop picking on Karen."

Grady was still regarding them all with confusion, but his wife looked as if she was about to burst into laughter at any second. Given Lauren's obviously unpredictable mood, Wade decided he'd better try to forestall that by getting their waitress over and their order placed.

As luck would have it, Cassie was working tonight. Her eyes widened, then turned speculative when she spotted Wade crowded into the booth next to Lauren.

"What's this?" she asked, clearly fascinated.

"Everybody having the meat loaf?" Wade inquired, ignoring Cassie's curious glance.

"I certainly am," Grady said.

"Me, too," Karen agreed.

"That makes three, then," Wade said. "Lauren, how about you?"

"I'll have a small green salad," she said.

He stared at her. "And?"

"That's it, just a small salad, please, Cassie. Dressing on the side."

"You've got it," Cassie said, and hurried away.

Wade didn't miss the way she immediately huddled with Stella by the kitchen door, or the way the owner's gaze promptly shifted in their direction. He grinned at Lauren, who was wearing an especially stormy expression.

"Looks like we're causing a stir," he noted, more amused by that than he would have been under other circumstances. The fact that Lauren was clearly irritated gave him a perverse sense of satisfaction.

"Yes, well, some people ought to mind their own damn business," she retorted.

Grady's eyes widened as he finally caught on to the sparks flying between Wade and Lauren. "Uh-oh. Karen, maybe you and I should move to that booth over there."

"Good idea," she said, abandoning them so fast it made Wade's head spin. Grady was right on her heels.

"Now look what you've done," Lauren said, scowling at him.

"Me? All I did was point out the obvious. Besides, it's your friends who are talking, not mine."

"Well, they wouldn't have anything to talk about if you'd just…"

"Just what? Ignored Grady's invitation and sat by myself?"

Flashing eycs met his. "Yes. As a matter of fact, that would have been just perfect."

"Really? Don't you think he would have wanted to know why? And since he has insisted we both make an effort to get along, do you think I should take the blame because you're being a spoiled brat?"

"Me? A spoiled brat?" Indignation turned her eyes an amazing shade of deep sparkling green.

Wade leaned back. "That's how it seems to me. You've ruined a perfectly pleasant evening for everyone by making your disdain for me plain."

For an instant she seemed genuinely taken aback by his assessment. "But I don't…" Her voice trailed off and her expression turned miserable. "I'm sorry."

"For?"

"Behaving like a spoiled brat, what else? It's just that you and I parted on a lousy note after a halfway-decent day. Then, after that, Karen ticked me off with a lot of nonsense about you and me. And now here you are, crowding me, and Cassie's looking as if she's just discovered the best-kept secret in Winding River, and I got testy, okay? I've already dealt with enough speculation to last me a lifetime. So sue me.''

"That's what I like,'' he said. "A heartfelt apology.''

When she lifted her downcast gaze and met his eyes, there was a jolt to his system. He had a hunch his heart couldn't take a lot of vulnerable looks like that.

"I'm sorry,'' she said again, and this time she sounded as though she meant it.

"So what was that comment about dealing with a lot of speculation all about?''

For a minute she looked so flustered, he was certain he must have hit on something sensitive, but then a cool mask slipped over her face so quickly, he was sure he must have imagined it.

"Did I say that?'' she said. "It's a small town. People talk. You know how it goes.''

Unfortunately, he did, so he let the subject drop. He grinned, then nodded in the direction of Grady and Karen, who were unabashedly watching the entire exchange. "Think we should invite them back over?''

"In the interest of peace and harmony, by all means,'' Lauren agreed at once. "Besides, it will keep them from falling off their seats trying to hear what we're saying.''

Wade glanced across the aisle and noted that Grady and Karen were, indeed, on the edge of the booth's benches, clearly trying to look uninterested in his conversation with Lauren.

"You have permission to return now,'' he said, amused by the flash of guilt on Grady's face and the eagerness on Karen's. She popped back across the aisle so fast, she almost tripped over her husband.

"Well?" she demanded. "Everything okay?"

"We've made peace," Lauren informed them.

Wade caught her gaze and added, "Again."

"You two making peace a lot?" Grady inquired.

Lauren nodded. "It seems to be our destiny."

Hearing that word in connection with the two of them gave Wade a bad moment. He didn't believe in destiny of any kind, especially not where women were concerned. Arlene had thought his father was *her* destiny, and look where that had gotten her. She'd been saddled with a bastard kid for the rest of her life. Even when he seethed with resentment toward his father, Wade could admit that it was Arlene who'd really gotten the raw deal. Her heart—and her spirit—had been irreparably broken.

Wade studiously avoided looking at the woman next to him and concentrated on his boss. "I went looking for those wild horses today."

The change of topic was so sudden that even Grady seemed taken aback, but he went along with it.

"And?" he said to Wade. "Find anything?"

"Not a sign of them."

"You don't suppose somebody's already rounded them up, do you?" Grady speculated.

Wade shook his head. "I would have heard about it."

Lauren frowned at him. "How? You're new in town."

"That doesn't mean I don't know how to keep my ear to the ground," he told her. "If somebody had gotten their hands on those horses, I'd have heard. Everybody knows I'm looking to build up our stock."

"*Our* stock? Since when did any of that stock start belonging to you?" Lauren asked.

"Actually, Wade owns a part interest in the horse operation," Grady said. "That was our deal."

She looked thoroughly surprised by the news. "Which one of you does Midnight actually belong to?"

"I bought him," Grady said. "He's got terrific bloodlines. You can see that by looking at him. Wade's hoping to breed him. We'll split up any foals he sires."

"But first I have to get him to stop kicking out at anything that gets within five feet of him," Wade said.

Lauren studied him with a blend of fascination and humor. "Which means you need me."

Wade feigned an exaggerated sigh. "So it seems."

A grin spread across her face. "What a perfectly lovely position for me to be in."

"Don't get too cocky, sweetheart. There are other people in the world who have a way with fractious horses."

"Maybe so, but none of them are me. Nor are they here. Right now, I'm all you've got." She reached up and patted his cheek. "Be nice to me."

The touch was no more than a two-second caress, but Wade's pulse took off like a stock car at Daytona. The woman was a sorceress. At this rate, she'd have him tamed right along with Midnight. He couldn't have that.

Before she could tuck her hand safely beneath the table, he caught it in midair and brought it to his lips. Gaze clashing with hers, he kissed her knuckles, lingering over the job until he felt her skin heat.

"A word of warning," he murmured.

"What?" she whispered, her voice suddenly shaky.

"You don't want to play with fire."

"Oh, my," a voice beside him murmured.

Wade looked up to find Cassie standing there with an armload of plates and a dazed expression. He grabbed a couple of the dinners before they wound up on the floor and passed them off to Karen and Grady, then took Lauren's salad and served it to her. By that time, Cassie had recovered enough to set his own plate in front of him.

She regarded Lauren with a questioning look. "Anything else?"

"Oh, I think that about does it," Lauren said wryly. "I'm apparently providing dinner and the entertainment. I hope everybody's happy."

Wade grinned at her. "I know I am."

Chapter Five

It took a lot to rattle Lauren, but Wade had managed to completely disconcert her the night before. As she sat on the porch sipping her morning coffee, she considered the entire encounter at Stella's. She wasn't sure which had shaken her more, her physical response to him or the discovery that he had a stake in the ranch's horses.

Since the latter was far less threatening to her personal equilibrium, she decided to deal with that first. Why had she been so surprised? Was it merely because Grady hadn't mentioned it? Or was it because she'd dismissed Wade as being nothing more than a ranch employee who served at Grady's discretion? Was she a snob—the spoiled brat that Wade had accused her of being?

No, she assured herself, that couldn't be. She had

the corral?'' Wade inquired, coming up on her from behind yet again.

Lauren frowned at him. ''I wish you'd stop sneaking up on me.''

''Hey,'' he said, looking wounded. ''I knocked on the kitchen door. When nobody answered, I came inside and shouted. Then I spotted you out here and came on out. I don't think that qualifies as sneaking.''

''Whatever,'' she said, refusing to get drawn into an argument as ridiculous as this one was turning out to be.

''So how about it? You working today?''

''As soon as I finish my coffee,'' she said, stubbornly staying right where she was. ''I can only spend an hour or so with Midnight, anyway.''

Wade nodded. ''True, but I have another horse you might want to take a look at. If you're interested.''

Feeling more eager than she wanted to be, Lauren forced a casual note into her voice. ''What's the problem?''

''I wish to heck I knew,'' Wade admitted with evident frustration. ''I bought her at a sale in Cheyenne a couple of months back. She seemed to be doing fine, but ever since we got here, she's been off her feed. The vet can't find anything wrong.''

''Then she's your horse, not Grady's?''

''Yes. Is that a problem? I'll pay whatever fee you set if you think you can help her.''

Lauren frowned at that. ''It's not about the money. I just like to know who I'm answering to.'' She stood up. ''Let's go take a look at her. But first I've got to stop in the kitchen and pick up some treats for Midnight.''

''If you bring a carrot for Miss Molly, you'll make

her day. That's the only thing she shows any interest in at all.''

She regarded him with amusement. ''Miss Molly?''

''My mom was a big fan of the golden oldies.''

She stared at him blankly.

'''Good Golly, Miss Molly.' Little Richard.''

To her amazement, he sang a few bars in a low voice that seemed to linger over the part about how good she looked to him. His gaze never left her face.

''I remember,'' she said, her voice a little choked. He was doing it again—charming her, tying her up in knots.

In the kitchen, she hurriedly sliced a couple of carrots into chunks, then followed Wade out the door.

''Should I count this as a sign of respect that you're letting me near your horse?'' she asked as they reached the barn.

''You wouldn't have gotten anywhere near Midnight a second time if I hadn't seen for myself that you know your way around horses,'' he claimed.

''I thought Grady ordered you to give me a chance.''

''He did, but I would have fought him tooth and nail if I'd thought there was any risk involved to the horses. As it was, I was more worried about the risk to you. There's a point when being intrepid and confident turns dangerous.''

His words made her heart flutter. She'd had directors blithely ask her to dangle from the side of a mountain with little concern for her safety. Here was a man she barely knew who'd been truly worried about her getting hurt even when he hadn't much liked her.

''Thank you…I think.''

''No problem,'' he said, shrugging off the thanks.

"Miss Molly's still in her stall. She won't leave it un-less I force her."

Lauren took the hint and fell into step beside him as he approached the pretty little bay filly. She was a beauty, all right. Perfectly proportioned for her size, she had a coat that gleamed in the weak rays of sun filtering through the window behind her.

"She's beautiful," Lauren said, then inched closer to the stall. "Aren't you, girl?"

The horse showed little interest in her or in Wade. She just stood there silently, head hanging. Even when Lauren extended a chunk of carrot on the palm of her hand, Miss Molly barely lifted her head to examine it. Finally, with little enthusiasm, the horse took the car-rot, chewed slowly, then turned her back on both of them to poke her head through the open window and gaze at the pasture beyond.

"What can you tell me about her?" Lauren asked Wade.

"Like I said, I bought her at a sale in Cheyenne. She was a spirited little thing, and she was training well. Then we came here and..." He shrugged. "You can see how she is."

"Where were you before? What was it like?"

"It was another ranch. The barn wasn't half as nice as this one."

"A lot of other horses?"

"No more than here." He regarded her curiously. "What are you thinking?"

Lauren hesitated to say. She was no expert in animal behavior. What she knew came from instinct and ex-perience—but Wade was actually regarding her with genuine attention, awaiting her verdict.

"Okay," she said finally. "This may sound crazy, but could she be homesick?"

A bark of laughter erupted before he could contain himself. "Homesick? She's a horse, not a college freshman. Besides, she wasn't in that barn all that long. How could she have gotten that attached to anything?"

Lauren reacted defensively to the instantaneous derision in his voice. "It was just a thought. Ignore it, if you think it's stupid." She whirled around and left the barn.

She was outside at the railing watching Midnight in the distance when Wade finally joined her.

"I'm sorry," he said gruffly.

"For?"

"I asked for your opinion. I had no right to make fun of it when you gave it."

"True," she agreed.

"So, let's say you could be right about this. What the hell do I do? Move back to the other ranch?"

"That seems a little extreme," she said, grinning at the frustration in his voice. "Let me think about it. Maybe I can come up with something less drastic."

"I hope so," he said, giving her another of those thoroughly disconcerting looks. "I'm just starting to like the scenery around here."

After several days Wade was forced to face the fact that he'd misjudged Lauren when he'd assumed she was nothing more than some pampered rich girl who was visiting the ranch on a lark. She had a head on her shoulders and a real knack with horses—all horses. She was like some kind of pied piper with them. Although she hadn't solved Miss Molly's problem yet, she was doing well with Midnight. He came to her almost eagerly now, which Wade could readily understand. The horse was male, wasn't he? And Lauren was every inch a female.

He was even more impressed by the way she pitched in and did chores in the barn without being asked. Did them like a woman who was familiar with them, too. She didn't seem to care how messy the chore was. She never complained about the heat, or the broken fingernails, or the straw that tangled in her hair.

At the end of the first week they'd spent working together, she stood before him, hands on hips, jeans filthy, her blouse damp, her cheeks flushed. "Anything else?" she asked.

Because he couldn't resist, because he was a fool, he murmured, "Only this," and claimed her mouth in a kiss that raised the temperature in the barn to a dangerous level. With all that flammable material around, it was a wonder the whole place didn't go up in flames.

Big mistake, he told himself the minute he managed to force himself to release her. Once a man had crossed that kind of line and discovered that the temptation was every bit as spectacular as it had promised to be, he was pretty much doomed to repeat it.

"What was that for?" Lauren asked eventually.

She was regarding him with a dazed expression that made him want to kiss her all over again. "I wish I knew," he muttered and walked off before she could start analyzing the kiss to death.

He worked himself to the point of exhaustion for the rest of the day. Unfortunately, nothing he did drove out the memory of his lips on hers, of the softness of her curves pressed against him.

"Fool," he muttered to himself a thousand times. It wasn't bad enough that she'd annoyed the daylights out of him—now he'd arranged it that she was going to plague him all the livelong night. A man who'd been celibate for as long as he had had no business kissing any female he didn't intend to take straight to bed.

As the night wore on, Wade's regrets grew. The taste of her was still with him. So was the heat, the restless yearning. He paced from one end of his three-room house to the other, then moved to the porch. When rocking proved no more relaxing, he headed for the main house, determined to catch a glimpse of her. Maybe a five-minute confrontation, the exchange of a few heated words would remind him of just why he'd had no business kissing Lauren in the first place. Since they rarely exchanged more than five civil words in a row, he figured the odds of a good verbal tussle were in his favor.

He found Lauren sitting on the front steps, wearing jeans and a tank top which should have been outlawed for a body like hers. How was a man supposed to think around a woman dressed like that? How was he supposed to start a halfway decent fight, when the urge to drag her right back into his arms was so powerful it took everything in him to resist it?

"Grady's inside," she said when she saw him.

"I didn't come to see Grady."

"Oh?"

Wade shoved his hands in his pockets and stood a careful distance away. "About this morning…"

The moonlight caught her face just right, and he was pretty sure he saw the beginning of a smile tugging at her lips. "Yes?"

"I had no right to do what I did."

"You mean kissing me?"

"Of course I mean kissing you," he snapped. Did

he have to spell everything out for her? "What else would I be apologizing for?"

There was no mistaking her grin now. "Is that what you were doing? Apologizing?"

"Yes, dammit."

"Must be a new experience," she said, laughter threading through her voice.

"Why is that?"

"Because you're not very good at it."

When he would have whirled around and stalked away, she added, "That's okay. No apology necessary. Just don't make a habit of it."

"Believe me, I won't," he said fervently. If today was any example of the aftermath, he was going to give her such a wide berth that they'd never even cross paths again. He'd leave notes telling her what he expected of her as far as the horses were concerned, then hightail it to some other part of the ranch. He could carve out some decent distance to keep between them if he put his mind to it.

"Want some iced tea?" she asked, cutting into his thoughts.

He stared at her. "What?"

This time she did laugh out loud. "It wasn't a trick question. It's a hot night. I asked if you wanted some iced tea—I brought a pitcher out with me. I can run in and get an extra glass."

Wade considered the friendly gesture. What could be the harm, especially now that he'd laid all his cards on the table? She knew there weren't going to be any more kisses. They both knew it. And he had a plan to stay out of her path from here on out. In the meantime, there was no reason not to stay for a few minutes of polite sociability.

"Sure," he said finally. "But I'll get the glass. I know where they are." Besides, the walk inside would give him a few minutes to cool off and shake the temptation to kiss her again. He figured it would set a very bad precedent if he kissed her not five minutes after swearing that he would never do it again.

She shrugged. "Whatever." She turned her gaze to the night sky as if what he did were of no consequence at all.

For some reason that annoyed Wade just as much as everything else Lauren did. He stalked past her, went into the kitchen and retrieved a glass. He was on his way back to the porch when Grady caught him in the front hall.

"You need something, Wade?"

"Just getting a glass," he said, relieved that the overhead light was off so his boss wouldn't see the color that was no doubt flaming in his cheeks.

"None down at your place?" Grady inquired, laughter threading through his voice.

Wade found himself clenching his teeth. "Actually, Lauren asked me to join her for a glass of iced tea."

"You two getting along better, then?"

"It's a constant test of our natural instinct to butt heads, but we're trying."

Grady nodded. "That's good. Well, you two enjoy yourselves."

He sounded too much like a father anxious to see his daughter settled down. Hearing that tone in his voice made Wade's skin crawl. "You could come on out and join us," he said, suddenly desperate for a buffer.

"Not me. I have plans, and they don't include the likes of you. Karen's upstairs."

How could he have forgotten that? It seemed as if sex was in the air tonight and there was no escaping it. "Yeah, right," Wade mumbled. "Well, see you tomorrow."

"Crack of dawn," Grady said. "We've got to move the herd to the west pasture."

Wade had completely forgotten that he'd offered to help out with that. "What about Lauren?"

"What about her?" Grady asked.

"Maybe I'd better tell her to spend the day shopping or something," Wade suggested.

What might have started out as a laugh suddenly turned into a cough. "Why don't you do that?" Grady said. "I think I'll come out after all and watch."

Wade sighed. "You don't think she'll go for it, do you?"

"I think she'll cut you up in little pieces and spit you out if you even suggest such a thing," Grady said cheerfully.

"It was just an idea. I don't want her around Midnight without someone to keep an eye on things."

"Then tell her what your concerns are and let her decide."

"Her?" Wade asked. "Lauren's impulsive and stubborn. She'll spend the whole blasted day with the horse just to spite me."

"Then it'll be her choice," Grady said.

Wade felt his stomach turn over. "And if we come back and find her lying in the dirt with a couple of cracked ribs or worse, will that be her choice, too?"

Grady's expression sobered. "You're really worried, aren't you? Aren't things going as well as I'd hoped they would?"

"Up to a point," Wade said cautiously. "But she's

the kind of woman who'll push the limits, and you know it.''

"Talk to her," Grady said again. "Lauren's a lot smarter than you're giving her credit for being. She's not going to do anything foolish unless you goad her into it.''

Wade scowled at having the responsibility for Lauren's actions placed squarely on his shoulders once again. "I'll talk to her,'' he said grimly. "Not that I think it'll do any good.''

He walked outside and let the screen door slam behind him, so he couldn't be accused of sneaking up on her again.

"Nice to know you have such a favorable impression of my common sense,'' Lauren said mildly.

Wade groaned. After her protests about how he was always sneaking around, it had never occurred to him that she could hear every word he and Grady had exchanged inside the house.

"Sorry,'' he mumbled.

"Are you really?'' she asked. "Or are you just sorry you got caught?''

"Mostly the latter,'' he said with candor. "I try never to insult a woman to her face.''

"Just behind her back?''

"If we're going to get into a sparring match over this, can I have some of that tea?'' he asked.

Lauren nodded toward the table. "There's the pitcher. Help yourself.''

Despite himself, he bit back a grin. He should have known she wasn't going to demean herself by waiting on him. He poured the tea, took a long swallow and tried to find some way to get his foot out of his mouth.

"Since you heard everything we said, I don't suppose there's any chance at all that you'll consider going over to Winding River tomorrow and spending the day shopping?'' he asked hopefully.

She beamed at him. ''Nope. Consistency is important when you're working with a horse. I need to stay right here.''

Because she was right, he didn't have a good argument for that. ''Will you at least promise to stay out of the corral, to keep the fence between you and Midnight?''

''Midnight is not going to hurt me.''

Wade's frustration mounted. ''Dammit, you don't know that. He was as good as wild a few weeks ago.''

''And he's trusting me more and more every day. You've seen it yourself.''

''I just don't want you getting overconfident and taking risks, especially with nobody else around,'' Wade insisted.

Her gaze met his and lingered. He saw the precise moment when curiosity was replaced by surprise. Her expression softened.

''This isn't some macho edict, is it?'' she asked, studying him. ''You're really worried about me.''

''I'm just not sure Grady and Karen have enough insurance to pay for patching your head back together,'' he insisted, refusing to admit that he cared the least little bit on his own behalf.

She reached for his hand. ''No, you're worried about me, aren't you, Wade? Admit it.''

He frowned at her persistence, but he wasn't going to lie. ''Okay, fine. Yes, I'm worried about you.''

''Why?''

Now that, he thought, was the sixty-four-thousand-dollar question. ''Because anything that has to do with the horses around here is my responsibility,'' he said finally.

''So, this is purely a selfish concern on your part,'' she said, her gaze still clashing with his, daring him to deny it.

''Yes,'' he insisted.

''Bull,'' she said softly. ''But I'll let it pass this time.''

She stood up, and the movement was enough to send the scent of her perfume wafting toward him. She put her hand on his cheek, then slowly withdrew it. ''Thanks for caring.''

She was gone before he could think of a satisfactory comeback.

''How did you and Wade make out last night?'' Grady inquired as he bolted down his breakfast at dawn the next morning.

Karen's gaze shot toward Lauren. ''You were with Wade last night?''

''He stopped by,'' Lauren said tightly. ''We talked for a while, though he and Grady actually had a much more fascinating conversation in the foyer.''

Dull red climbed into Grady's cheeks. ''Damn!''

Lauren grinned at him. ''It's nice that you took my side. And actually it's rather sweet that Wade's so worried about me, even if it is annoying that he doesn't trust me to have a grain of sense in my head.''

Karen listened, looking spellbound by the entire exchange. ''My, my. Wade's sweet *and* annoying, all in one breath. Where was I when all this was going on?''

''Tucked into bed waiting for your husband,'' Lauren said. ''See what happens when you have a one-track mind? You miss all the fun stuff that goes on around here.''

Karen's gaze flew to meet her husband's, and her cheeks flushed. "Oh, I don't know about that."

Lauren groaned. "I'm going to the barn. If the horses have the hots for each other, at least I don't have to hear about it."

"But *I* want to hear every last detail about you and Wade," Karen called after her. "I won't forget about this."

Lauren sighed. "Yes, I know. It's one of those sad truths I've come to accept. You're the worst meddler in our crowd, and I have the misfortune to be living right under your nose."

"You could move in with Wade," Grady suggested, trying to look innocent and failing miserably.

"What have I done to myself?" Lauren asked with a resigned sigh. "You're as bad as she is."

"Actually, we're a helluva team," Karen said. "Face it, sweetie, you're doomed."

"I refuse to accept that," Lauren said adamantly.

Karen grinned. "I know. That's why this is so much fun."

Chapter Six

Lauren was almost at the barn when she heard a car pull up, then the sharp sound of two doors slamming. She turned back just in time to spot Emma and her daughter, Caitlyn, heading her way. Emma waved at Lauren, but all of the child's attention was focused on the horses in the corral.

"Hey, there," Lauren called out. "What brings you two out this way?"

"Caitlyn wanted to visit her aunt Karen's horses," Emma claimed with a perfectly straight face. "She's been obsessed with them ever since her grandfather gave her that pony. And now that she's seven—"

"I'm almost eight," Caitlyn corrected.

Emma gave Lauren a rueful smile. "Excuse me. Now that she's almost eight, she wants a grown-up horse."

Lauren shook her head. The explanation might be

true enough as far as it went, but there was more. Workaholic Emma wouldn't have made the drive on a weekday just to satisfy her daughter's whim. Nope, this was all about Emma's curiosity, which had clearly been fanned by reports of the events of two nights ago from Cassie or Stella or both.

"Nice try," Lauren said to Emma, "but there are plenty of horses at your folks' place. What's the real reason you're here? Or should I even bother to ask?"

"Okay, the truth? We wanted to check up on you," Emma said, still feigning innocence. "How are you settling in?"

Lauren took one look at the amusement glinting in Emma's eyes and sighed. That look went way beyond casual interest. She definitely knew something—or thought she did.

"What have you heard?" Lauren asked, resigned to a cross-examination.

"Heard?" Emma asked, though her innocent expression was wavering. "Is there something to hear?"

Lauren frowned. "To borrow an expression from an attorney who used to be among my best friends, go suck an egg."

Emma laughed. "Then it's true? You *were* getting all nice and cozy with Grady's new wrangler at Stella's the night before last? That was the first thing I heard over coffee this morning. Cassie couldn't wait to spill the beans."

"Define cozy," Lauren said. "We were with Karen and Grady, after all. And is this something we should be discussing in front of your daughter?"

Actually Caitlyn was already inching toward the rail at the corral and was pretty much out of earshot.

Emma chuckled. "Speaking of nice tries," she said.

"But you're not getting away with it, either. Caitlyn is far more interested in the horses than she is in anything we have to say. Now talk to me. What's the deal? Who is this guy? What do you know about him? How involved are the two of you?"

"There's nothing to tell," Lauren said. "That's my story and I'm sticking to it."

Emma's gaze suddenly shifted away. "Hmm? Could this be the man in question coming our way? Maybe *he'll* be more talkative."

Lauren spun around and shot a warning look in Wade's direction. "Stay away," she shouted.

He regarded her with confusion. "Why?"

"Because Emma has questions, and she's a seasoned trial attorney. She'll grill you until you tell her what she wants to know."

She should have guessed that that was the exact wrong thing to say. Wade hesitated, then closed the distance despite her warning. If anything, he looked intrigued.

"I have nothing to hide," he said. "What's the crime?"

"No crime," Lauren said, resigned to the inevitable. "Emma has heard things about the two of us."

Wade looked nonplussed by that, but he was too close now to turn tail and run. Not that he would have, anyway, she realized. He'd already done his part at Stella's to keep the talk alive. He was clearly enjoying either her discomfort or being the center of attention himself.

"Fascinating," he said now. "According to these reports, was I any good?"

Emma shifted her gaze to Lauren. "Now that *is* fascinating. My sources didn't seem to know that things had gone that far.''

"*Things,* as you so eloquently put it, haven't gone anywhere at all," Lauren said. "Wade's just trying to stir up the pot. He seems to find it amusing, while I, to the contrary, have had my fill of people dissecting my life. In no time at all, it gets out of hand.''

Emma's expression sobered at once. "Sorry. I wasn't thinking. You're right. Of all people, I should know better. I've had my own share of run-ins with the media. I know how quickly things can get out of hand.''

"Media?" Wade said, picking up on the telling remark at once. "Why would they be involved? I thought this was about small-town gossip.''

Lauren shot a discouraging look at Emma, then told Wade, "Emma had a bad encounter with the Denver press.'' Perhaps she could shift all of the focus to Emma and away from her own experiences.

"Aren't you Ford Hamilton's wife now?" Wade asked Emma. "You must have gotten over it, if you decided to marry the editor of the local paper.''

"I trust my husband," Emma agreed. "But not the media in general.''

He nodded. "Fair enough. But what does any of that have to do with Lauren?''

"It's not important," Lauren said hurriedly. "Did you need me for something?''

He stared at her blankly for a minute, then nodded. "Oh, yeah, I was going to let you know that I'm leaving now. I'll be gone most of the day. Remember what we talked about.''

"My memory's not that short," she said testily. "I

don't need to be reminded that you don't trust my judgment.''

''Lauren—''

''I know, I know. I won't do anything stupid.''

He gave a curt nod of satisfaction. ''That's good. I'll hear about it if you do.''

''Who's going to tell? Midnight? Is the horse conversing with you now?''

''Dammit, Lauren, this isn't a game,'' he said with evident frustration. ''He's still dangerous.''

No sooner were the words out of his mouth than Lauren heard Caitlyn calling out to an approaching horse. She turned just in time to see Midnight dancing closer to the child, who had climbed atop the split-rail fence. Midnight was probably braving the encounter with the hope of getting one of the treats Lauren had been bringing him on a daily basis.

Wade spotted the potential for tragedy at precisely the same moment. Before Lauren could even begin to gather her wits, he was across the ground scooping Caitlyn into his arms and out of the horse's reach. Caitlyn was scowling at her abrupt removal.

''Why'd you do that?'' she demanded, regarding Wade with a disapproving pout. She was completely oblivious to the danger she'd been in.

Wade grinned at her to take the sting out of his action. ''Because Midnight's scared of pretty little girls.''

The pout faded and Caitlyn's eyes widened with interest. ''That great big horse is scared of *me?*''

''Yes, indeed,'' Wade confirmed.

Caitlyn still looked doubtful. ''He didn't look scared.''

Emma turned to Lauren, a question in her eyes.

"The problem horse I've been working with," Lauren mouthed quietly.

The color drained out of Emma's face. She gathered Caitlyn out of Wade's arms and hugged her so hard the child protested.

"Mommy, stop!"

"Sorry, baby, for a minute there you had me scared, too," Emma said, then lifted her gaze to Wade. "Thank you."

He shrugged. "Not a problem. It probably would have been fine, but it's better to be safe than sorry," he said, with a pointed look at Lauren.

"I'll use my head," she promised. "Now go. Grady needs your help this morning. He's probably chomping at the bit to get started."

Wade nodded, and after one more long look, he turned on his heel, mounted his horse and rode off.

"My, my," Emma murmured when he'd gone. "I see what Cassie was talking about. The sparks between you two are better than the Fourth of July fireworks."

Caitlyn picked up on her mother's remark and regarded Lauren seriously. "Is he your boyfriend, Aunt Lauren?"

"Absolutely not," Lauren said heatedly.

But the idea was beginning to hold more appeal than she cared to admit. And seeing Wade with Caitlyn cradled protectively against his chest had certainly helped to enhance that appeal.

Wade still got nauseous when he thought of what could have happened to Caitlyn if Midnight had gotten fractious when she was within inches of his hooves earlier. He couldn't seem to shake that image.

Nor was he able to shake the probability that Lauren

would deliberately defy him today, despite her promise. He didn't trust that promise any more than he'd ever trusted his mother's promise that one day his rich daddy was going to come for them. The bad feeling in the pit of his stomach wasn't going to go away until he got back to the ranch and found Lauren in one piece.

"What's on your mind?" Grady asked, riding up alongside him as they slowly made their way home after the long, hard day. "Or should I ask who?"

"Look, you're the one who made Lauren's safety my concern," Wade grumbled. "Is it any wonder I keep thinking about all the mischief she could have gotten into while we were gone today?"

"Didn't she agree that she wouldn't try anything dangerous?" Grady asked reasonably.

"Yes, but her definition of dangerous and mine would probably differ significantly."

"She won't go back on her word," Grady insisted.

"If you say so," Wade said, unable to hide his skepticism.

"You don't trust easily, do you?"

"Never had any reason to," Wade said. "Too damn few of the people in my life ever kept their word."

"I'm sorry," Grady told him with genuine sympathy. "That must have been a helluva way to grow up."

Wade shrugged. "It's a lesson every man needs to learn sooner or later. I just caught on sooner than most."

"You're wrong about that," Grady insisted. "Most people are honest and caring and trustworthy, if you give 'em half a chance."

"You can afford to say that with people like your grandfather and Karen in your life." Wade knew that Grady's grandfather, Thomas Blackhawk, was an honorable man. He'd heard a lot of stories about him since coming to the ranch, though he had yet to meet the sage Native American. As for Karen, she'd treated Wade with nothing but kindness and respect. He could believe she was an exception to his rule, too.

"Lauren's one of Karen's best friends," Grady pointed out. "Do you honestly think they'd be close if Lauren weren't cut from the same cloth? That whole gang of them—they call themselves the Calamity Janes—are loyal to a fault. Keep that in mind in case you're ever tempted to do anything that might hurt Lauren."

Wade sighed at the warning. He wasn't going to win this argument about trustworthiness. In fact, he wasn't even sure he wanted to. A part of him prayed that Grady was right about Lauren, but it was way too soon for him to put any faith in her yet. Her behavior while he'd been gone today might be a start toward convincing him, though.

"Keep an open mind," Grady urged as they rode toward the house. "That's all I'm saying."

Wade nodded. "I'll do my best."

But when he walked into the barn, he found it disconcerting to see Lauren wearing dirt-streaked jeans, dusty boots and a blouse that looked as if she'd been wrestling a hog. She hadn't gotten into that state by sitting on her pretty little derriere in the ranch office all day long or sipping lemonade on the porch. So much for honor and trust, he thought.

"Tough day?" he inquired mildly, leaning against the doorjamb and studying her intently to see if there was any evidence of scrapes or bruises to go along with the general disarray.

Her gaze shot up to clash with his, and her expression turned defiant. "Quite productive, actually."

"Oh?"

"I had a little test of wills with a certain horse."

Wade's temper soared. Absolute panic lodged in his throat, even though he could see perfectly well that whatever she'd done, she was still in one piece. If she had any injuries, they weren't obvious.

He shoved away from the door and began to pace. "Dammit, Lauren, I warned you to stay the hell away from Midnight. Whatever possessed you to defy me the second my back was turned, especially after you'd promised to do as I asked?" He glared at her. "Typical female. You just had to have your own way, didn't you? Answer me this. Is Midnight all right?"

She returned his gaze evenly, though the color in her cheeks was high. "Midnight is just fine, you idiot. And I did not defy you. It was Miss Molly who objected to joining me for a little ride around the corral."

Wade stopped in his tracks. "Miss Molly did this? She threw you?"

"Five times," Lauren confirmed.

He muttered a soft curse. "You don't catch on quick, do you?"

"I was going to give her ten chances, but she came through for me on the sixth try," Lauren said, her expression tired but triumphant. "We reached an agreement. One trip around the corral and she got carrots for dessert tonight."

Wade strode over so that he could examine her more closely. Except for the dishevelment, she looked just fine. "You're really okay?"

"My butt may not be the same for a while, but other than that, I'm fine."

He shoved a hand through his hair. "I didn't expect you to get this far with her this fast."

"Well, she seemed docile enough when I led her out of her stall. I thought the ride would go fine." She shrugged. "I was wrong."

"How is she now?"

Her expression fell then. "I wish I could tell you that this had solved everything, but it didn't. She went straight into her stall, ignored her feed and turned her back on me. Reminds me of a kid trying to make a point after being forced to eat his spinach. At least she got some exercise today. Maybe tomorrow will be better."

Wade was torn between his desire to check on his horse and his longing to touch the woman standing in front of him. Once all of the anger and panic had drained away, he'd been left with this insatiable need to hold her. Because that was a really bad idea, he backed away and went to see Miss Molly.

The horse was standing quietly in her stall, looking as dejected as ever. Her ears twitched when he approached, but she made no move to come to him.

"So, I hear you had yourself quite a time today, girl," he said, reaching over the gate and rubbing a hand along her neck. She shuddered at the touch and gazed at him with those liquid brown eyes that had seemed so sad the last few weeks. "You know Lauren's just trying to help you. It's not very polite to toss her on her butt over and over again."

He dug a handful of carrot chunks out of his pocket and held one out. Miss Molly nuzzled his palm, then took it. Once she'd daintily chewed that piece, she nudged him for more. He gave her a couple, then put the rest back in his pocket.

"Okay, beggar, that's enough. I know Lauren's been sneaking carrots to you, too. She said that's how she paid you off for your cooperation today. Next time, though, she might not be so generous."

Miss Molly whinnied, then pulled her head back into the stall and turned away from him. Clearly, without the bribe of carrots, she wanted no part of him.

Thoroughly frustrated by the horse's lackluster attitude, Wade stepped back, muttering another heartfelt curse.

"Strong words just because you didn't get your way," Lauren noted calmly.

"It's not about getting my way," he protested. "It's about seeing a terrific animal losing her spirit like this. It's like something sucked all the life out of her." When Lauren seemed about to say something, he frowned. "Don't start on that homesick nonsense again."

"Is it really such a crazy idea?" she asked. "Horses have emotions, too. They get attached to people and other horses. Think about it. Was there anyone at the old ranch who spent a lot of time with her? Did she have a stablemate that was always turned out to pasture with her?"

"No," Wade retorted, unable to conceal his impatience. "Maybe I should get the vet out here again."

"That's up to you," Lauren said with a shrug. "But I think you're wasting your money."

Wade wasn't going to stand here and discuss her ridiculous idea another minute, not when he couldn't seem to drag his gaze away from the streak of dirt on her pale cheek or the strands of straw stuck in her hair.

"Come here," he murmured.

She blinked and stared. "Why?"

He grinned and hoisted himself onto the gate of an empty stall. "I'm not going to bite. Come over here."

She took a cautious step closer, and then another. "What is it?"

Grinning now, Wade beckoned her closer. Once she was standing right in front of him, he tugged a clean handkerchief from his back pocket and wiped the smudge from her cheek. He noted with satisfaction that her amazing eyes went wide at the gesture. Cupping her chin in his hand, he reached for the straw, then brushed the wayward curls away from her face. He felt her tremble when his knuckles grazed her soft skin.

"That's better," he said when he was done. She started to back away, but he placed his hands on her shoulders and kept her right smack between his splayed thighs. "Are you sure you're okay?"

"Okay?" she whispered, her expression dazed.

"All those spills didn't bruise you, did they?"

"Oh," she murmured, then gave him a rueful grin. "I am a little sore, but I haven't checked out the part I landed on in a mirror yet."

He managed a perfectly serious expression. "I could check it for you," he offered with what he hoped was just the right touch of magnanimity.

She laughed then. "You wish."

He returned her gaze solemnly. "Yeah, I do."

She seemed totally taken aback by his honesty. "What are you saying, Wade?"

He swallowed hard and forced himself to say it. "I want you. God knows I don't want to, but I do."

The reply made her frown. "If it makes you this uncomfortable, maybe you should keep fighting the urge."

"Probably should," he agreed, allowing his thumbs

to begin a slow massage of the petal-soft skin along her collarbone. He caught the pulse jumping at his touch, the quick rise of heat in her cheeks. "But then I ask myself why we should deny ourselves something that promises to be so incredible."

He dared a bolder caress, a skimming touch that traced the curve of her breast, flicking across the peak in a way that left it pebble-hard against her blouse. He heard the hitch of her breath, caught the unmistakable flare of desire in her eyes. His own body was rock-hard with anticipation, the bulge in his jeans unmistakable. He watched her eyes go even darker when she caught sight of it.

"Wade?"

He wasn't entirely certain if it was a question or a plea. He smoothed her hair back, then rubbed his thumb across her lower lip. His own pulse began to pound when she stunned him by drawing his thumb into her mouth and sucking on it.

The game had started out of a sense of yearning he didn't quite know how to handle. Now it had turned serious, and while he knew the rules of this particular game, knew the moves that brought pleasure and the dangerous pitfalls of playing, he couldn't predict which of them would win. Maybe both of them would. Maybe it didn't even matter. Maybe, for now, it was just about the game itself.

He drew her closer, tighter, until she was pressed against the heat of his arousal. For an instant that was enough. But then an agony of wanting tore through him, even as she reached up and dragged his head down until his mouth met hers in a crushing kiss.

From the moment they'd met, from the first fiery exchange of words, he'd known that Lauren was a passionate woman, but he hadn't expected both of them to go up in flames so fast, so furiously. She was tugging frantically at his shirt, at the buckle on his belt, skimming nails over bare skin. He peeled off her blouse and bra in a single move that sent buttons flying and left the clothes in a tangled heap somewhere in the barn.

They were committed to the game now, no question about that. Her soft little moans were enough to heat a statue and bring it to life. Her caresses were brazen, catching him off guard and stealing his breath and any last lingering shred of sanity.

He slid down from his perch on the stall door, scooped her up and carried her inside to the bed of clean straw. He stripped off his shirt and laid it down, then slowly lowered her. She never hesitated at the makeshift bed, earning his respect and his undying gratitude. He wasn't sure he could have made it all the way to his house without exploding with this neediness she stirred in him. Thank heaven for the condom tucked in his wallet. Hopefully it hadn't dry-rotted from old age.

Lauren was already wriggling out of her jeans, no easy task since they got hung up on her boots. Wade refrained from chuckling at the ungraceful effort.

"Hey," he said, drawing her attention. "What say we slow this down?"

"No," she said tersely, tugging impatiently at a boot.

Something in her voice set off an alarm. The urgency of desire was one thing. Panic was quite another.

"Lauren, what's the hurry?"

She did hesitate then. The confusion in her eyes came close to breaking his heart, to say nothing of its effect on his libido.

"You afraid of changing your mind?" he asked.

She closed her eyes and went limp, then sighed and looked straight into his eyes. "Maybe."

"Then we don't do this," he said, managing a calm note despite the protest raging through his blood. "It's as simple as that."

"But I want you," she insisted.

"I know. That's plain enough," he said, caressing her cheek. "Just not as much as I want you. I can wait."

She moaned and fell back against the straw. "I'm going to be up all night because you're being so damn noble," she muttered.

He grinned at the evident frustration in her voice. "Join the club. How about we do dinner instead? Maybe a nice bottle of wine or a couple of beers will settle us both down."

Her gaze narrowed. "Who's cooking?"

"I will."

"You cook?"

"I can, if you're not too particular about what you eat. How does a western omelette sound?"

"Heavenly," she said at once.

He lifted himself up and went in search of her blouse and bra before he could act on the wicked ideas still raging through him. "Sorry about the blouse," he said when he handed it to her. "I'll buy you a replacement."

"You will," she agreed, then grinned. "Something with snaps."

Wade laughed. "Good idea." He held out a hand and helped her up. "Now scoot, before these noble intentions of mine lose out to my hormones."

"Your place in a half hour?" she asked.

''Perfect,'' he agreed.

Okay, maybe not so perfect, he thought as he headed home. How the hell was he supposed to keep his hands to himself all evening long, now that he knew exactly how Lauren felt beneath his touch?

Chapter Seven

Lauren spent ten of the precious thirty minutes Wade had granted her down in the barn trying to make herself presentable in case she ran into Grady or Karen up at the house. She didn't want either of them to take one look at her and conclude that she and Wade had been rolling around in the hay. Which, of course, they had been. Unfortunately—from her perspective—they had stopped short of making love.

Okay, maybe it *wasn't* unfortunate. Wade had seen what she hadn't been willing to admit. She wasn't ready to make the kind of commitment that would go along with that kind of intimacy. More important, she wasn't sure Wade was ready for any kind of commitment at all.

If she were a different person, maybe it wouldn't have mattered. They could have spent a few wonderfully wicked hours in each other's arms, then gone right along as if nothing momentous had happened. Sadly, though, Lauren had learned that she was really lousy at casual sex. Come to think of it, she wasn't much better with committed relationships, either, she reminded herself. She had two divorces to attest to that.

Of course, maybe the reason she'd jumped into those marriages had been the belief that commitment and sex went hand in hand, an anti-free-love morality, as it were. Maybe this time she should try to separate the two and not assume that just because she and Wade had all this delicious chemistry between them, they were suited to making a lifetime commitment.

"Well, hell," she muttered as she tried to make sense of it and couldn't.

She tied the ends of her blouse together in a knot that would at least give the illusion it was meant to be worn without buttons. As long as she didn't make any sudden movements or quick turns, it should get her past any inquisitive gazes.

En route to the house, Lauren went back over her quandary. If she wasn't any good at casual sex and was no better at marriage, what was left? She had a feeling she'd better figure that out in a hurry, since the heat between her and Wade wasn't something she could ignore forever. They were going to land in bed together. The only question left was on what terms? It was one thing to have a relationship end messily in Hollywood, quite another to stir up talk in Winding River.

As she neared the house, she could hear Grady and Karen in the kitchen, so she slipped around to the front door and fled up the steps. Once she'd washed her face, put on a light dusting of fresh makeup and brushed her hair, she felt marginally better. Clean clothes accomplished the rest. By the time she went downstairs, she was prepared to make a quick dash right back out the front door.

She'd almost made it, too, when Karen planted herself squarely in her path.

"Going somewhere, Lauren?" her friend inquired cheerfully, a glint in her eyes. "Don't think for a second that I didn't see you sneaking around the house and creeping upstairs hoping that we wouldn't see you. Now, here you go again, trying to slip out the front door undetected." She glanced toward Grady, who was watching the entire scene with amusement. "I think she's trying to keep something from us, don't you?"

"Looks that way," he agreed.

"If I had to guess, I'd say she has a hot date," Karen noted, surveying Lauren intently.

"I'm wearing old jeans and a T-shirt. Why would you think that?" Lauren demanded, totally perplexed by the assumption. "There is nothing remotely 'hot' about this outfit."

"Maybe not on the average woman, but on you?" Grady said. "I've got to go with Karen on this one."

Lauren frowned at him. "Oh, for Pete's sake, I'm running over to grab a quick bite with Wade. That's it. No mystery. No big romance. Just dinner."

Grady's eyebrows rose. "At his place?"

"Yes, why not? Is that some sort of big deal?"

Karen grinned and rolled her eyes. "She's going to a man's place and he's cooking, and she wants to know if it's a big deal? Girl, you have been out of circulation too long. It is a very big deal."

"He's fixing an omelette, not serving caviar and champagne," Lauren retorted irritably.

Grady suddenly looked worried. "Lauren, is that

what it's going to take to impress you? Caviar and champagne? I don't think Wade's that kind of guy."

"He's not, thank heavens," she agreed fervently. "Now if you two will stop hovering, I can go over there before dinner's ruined."

"Seems anxious," Karen teased.

"Very anxious," Grady agreed.

"You know, as two people who spend every spare second sneaking off to their bedroom, you may not have the best qualifications to act like a couple of nosy chaperons," Lauren pointed out. "If you're not careful, Wade and I might decide to keep you company every single evening from here on out."

Grady wrapped his arms around Karen's waist from behind. "Let her go," he said at once.

Karen laughed. "By all means."

Lauren darted out the front door, pretending that she didn't hear the hoots of laughter that followed her. That was the trouble with two people knowing her as well as Grady and Karen did—they thought they could get away with anything. After all, she had popped up repeatedly during their courtship. One of these days, though, Lauren was going to get even with them for tonight. She just had to come up with a plan diabolical enough. Maybe the rest of the Calamity Janes would help—although more than likely they'd be on Karen and Grady's side. They were all born meddlers. Heck, she'd been one herself up till now.

As Lauren neared Wade's house, her footsteps slowed. Memories of the heat she and Wade had generated earlier in the barn flushed her skin. Was she expecting a repeat of that tonight? Hoping for it?

"Dinner's going to be burned if you stand out there too much longer."

Wade's voice carried on the still night air, startling her. She could barely see him in the shadows, his feet propped on the porch railing.

"Sorry, I got sidetracked by Grady and Karen," she muttered as she joined him.

"Which doesn't explain why you were just standing out here," he teased. "Scared to come inside?"

The accurate accusation grated. A flash of temper came and went in a heartbeat. "That just makes me smart," she said.

"Oh? How so?"

She forced herself to meet his gaze without blinking. "Because of what happened in the barn a little while ago. We agreed we were going a little too fast. Now here we are alone together again, with all that energy still charging around in the atmosphere."

He grinned. "Then it *is* still charging around for you, too? I was afraid it was just me. I took the coldest shower I've ever taken in my life, and then you waltz across the yard and I'm so hot I could haul you straight off to bed right now."

Lauren swallowed hard at the temptation that shot through her. "We had a deal," she reminded him.

He sighed heavily. "I was afraid you were going to bring that up. Leave it to you to test a man's honor. Oh, well, come on inside and let's eat. We'll have a pleasant, quiet dinner and then discuss the rest."

She grinned despite herself. "You, a man of action, intend to discuss whether or not we have sex?"

"Hey, I'm a reasonable guy. I'm willing to look at all sides of the issue."

"I'll hold you to that."

When he led the way inside, carefully keeping his hands to himself, Lauren looked around curiously. It was a typical, simply decorated ranch outbuilding—a cottage, really—with masculine colors and a few over-size pieces of furniture suited to big men. The only personal touch she could see was a small framed pic-ture of a woman, her arms wrapped around the waist of a grinning boy. There was no mistaking that the boy was a younger version of Wade.

"Is this your mother?" she asked him.

He glanced at the picture, then nodded.

"She's beautiful."

The comment seemed to startle him. "Yeah, I sup-pose she is."

"What about your father?" she asked, then saw at once that it was the wrong thing to bring up. His jaw clenched visibly at the mention of his father, and his hands bunched into fists.

"Never knew him," he said tersely. "It was just my mother and me." He turned away and began cooking the diced onions and peppers in the omelette pan on the stove. He focused so hard on his actions, Lauren was surprised all the circuits in his brain didn't burn up.

"I'm sorry," she said, hoping to smooth things over.

"Nothing to be sorry for. It's just the way it was," he said, his grim expression belying the casual tone. "We did okay."

"Where is your mother now?"

"Still working at the same bar in Billings."

Lauren debated her next question, then decided to ask anyway. She needed to know what made Wade tick, and the only way to get to the truth was to push the boundaries, even when the topic clearly made him uncomfortable. "Is that where she met your father?"

He turned and scowled at her. "Why do you care about this?"

"Because you're not as blasé about it as you want me to believe. What do you know about him?"

"I know that he was a no-good son of a bitch who used my mother, then paid her off, rather than deal with the consequences. She wasn't the first woman Blake Travis used and discarded, and she likely wasn't the last. That's what his kind do."

Wade's bitterness cut straight through her. "His kind?"

"The rich and powerful. They take whatever they want. They're users. Give me someone who does an honest day's work for an honest day's pay any time."

Lauren felt her gut tighten at the depth of his anger toward an entire category of people. Worse, in his eyes, she was probably a part of that very category. He just didn't know it. How would he feel about her once he learned the obscene amount of money she made for what must seem like play to the uninitiated?

"Grady's rich, but he's not like that," she pointed out, testing the waters with an example less risky than herself.

"No," he agreed. "Grady seems to be a decent guy. I have no complaints where he's concerned, but I also have no illusions. He's got money and he's got power. His grandfather's a politician and a Native American activist. I'm an employee here, not Grady's pal."

She stared at him in shock. "You've got to be kidding. Grady respects you. He likes you. What would ever give you the idea that he doesn't consider you his equal in every way?"

"That's just the way it is," he said, his mouth set

in a tight line. "We get along fine as long as I don't cross that invisible line between us."

"If Grady was like that, do you think he'd approve of me being here with you tonight?"

He hesitated, then shrugged, dismissing the question. "It's not up to him. He probably knows he can't control you."

"Talk about being prejudiced," she accused. "That's the worst case of reverse snobbery I've ever heard."

He shrugged off the accusation. "Well, that's who I am. Take me or leave me."

"What if I were to tell you that I'm rich?"

He laughed as if it were the most ludicrous idea he'd ever heard. "For starters, I wouldn't believe it."

"Why not?" she probed, curious about exactly how he'd reached the conclusion that she didn't belong to a class of people he despised.

"Because you're living off the kindness of the Blackhawks, for one thing. And you work as hard as anybody else, no matter how filthy or demanding the job."

"Thank you," she said, even though he was only half-right. She did work hard. What was he going to do, though, when he found out the rest was wrong, that she was as rich as Grady and then some? She should tell him, right here and now. Get the truth out in the open and force him to deal with it. Or not.

It was the latter that made her hesitate. Wade was the best man to come into her life in a long time. She didn't want to risk losing him over something as trivial to her as the amount of money in her bank account. In time, when and if their relationship was on solid ground, she would tell him everything—about her career, her money, her marriages.

"You went quiet all of a sudden," he said as he set a plate in front of her. "Something you want to say?"

She shook her head. "Nothing. I could debate you all night on the absurdity of your bias, but I can see I'd be wasting my breath."

He nodded. "You certainly would." He held up a bottle of white wine and a beer. "What's your pleasure?"

"Beer," she said at once, then realized she'd done it in some mistaken attempt to prove that she wasn't some sort of elitist who only sipped wine with her meals. She refused to be somebody she wasn't just to avoid a conflict with his prejudice. "No, actually, I'd prefer the wine."

"No problem," he said easily, opening the bottle and pouring a glass for her. He popped the top on the beer for himself and drank it from the bottle.

Maybe he hadn't intended it that way, but Lauren saw it as a defiant gesture, an attempt to prove just how down-to-earth—how different from the rich and powerful—he was. Maybe it was even an unconscious attempt to put some distance between them. She stared at him over the rim of her glass.

"It's not going to work, you know."

His startled gaze met hers. "What?" he asked.

"The attempt to remind me what a badass kind of guy you are."

His lips twitched. "Is that what I'm doing? How?"

"The tough talk. Swigging your beer down straight from the bottle. Grady does the same thing. So do most of the men around here, rich or poor. I'm used to it. As you've already learned, character and money don't necessarily go hand in hand. You can be poor and still be an honorable, decent guy. Or you can be rich as Midas and be a creep, like your father.''

She studied him intently. "Or is it really your contention that *only* the poor, struggling working man can be decent? And that *all* the rich must be jerks?''

"When you put it that way, it does sound like a gross generalization,'' he admitted grudgingly. "Still, I've learned the hard way to watch my step around anyone with the big bucks. It's better to steer clear than to be taken advantage of. If you don't give them the opportunity, they can't use you.''

Now it was Lauren's turn to sigh. "You're not going to give an inch on this, are you?''

"Nope.''

"Then I'll save it for another day when you're feeling more reasonable.''

"Hell will freeze over first.''

He said it with a ferocity that stunned Lauren. The words sent a chill over her. In that instant, she had a terrible premonition that they were doomed before they ever really got started.

Wade sat at the table in his kitchen, sipping on his long-neck bottle of beer, and watched the mood deteriorate right before his eyes. He had no clue why Lauren seemed to take such offense at his attitude about the rich. She seemed to be taking it personally. Surely, in her experiences in California, she had butted up against plenty of wealthy people who treated lesser mortals the way his daddy had treated his mother. Heck, the way he saw it, that place must be the capital of the egomaniacal rich.

"Let's shift gears for a minute,'' he suggested eventually, hoping to recapture the earlier mood of easy camaraderie. "Why don't you tell me about your life in California?"

Rather than seizing on it as the neutral topic he'd hoped for, though, she tensed perceptibly.

"My life in California is over. I'm back in Wyoming to stay," she said, sounding every bit as defensive as he had earlier.

"Why did you go there in the first place?"

"I told you before—it seemed like it would be exciting," she said.

"And it wasn't?"

"It was," she said. "For a while."

His gaze narrowed at her terse replies. "Why don't you want to talk about it?"

"Because it doesn't matter," she said.

"It's part of who you are," he corrected.

"The same way your father and his actions are a part of who *you* are. You didn't want to talk about that, any more than I want to discuss a period of my life I've put behind me."

He studied her. There was usually only one reason a woman ran from her past, a man. "Who was he?" he asked eventually, not even sure he wanted to hear the answer.

She regarded him blankly. "Who was who?"

"The man who hurt you."

Her mouth curved in the beginnings of a smile. "What makes you think there was a man involved?"

"When a woman's as beautiful as you are, there usually is. Of course, usually it's the man who winds up brokenhearted."

"Your mother being the exception to that rule," she said, deliberately taunting him.

Wade frowned. He was forced to admit that she had pegged that right. "Yes," he said, his voice tight.

"Well, I hate to disappoint you, but no man chased me off. I came back here because I finally figured out that this is where I belong."

Wade regarded her with disbelief. "Really? What led you to reach this earth-shattering conclusion?"

"Ever since our class held its reunion a little over a year ago, I've been coming back to visit my friends," she explained. "I finally realized that I'm happier here than I was in Los Angeles. It's as simple as that."

She was holding something back. He could hear it in her cautious choice of words, see it in her eyes. "What aren't you telling me, Lauren?"

She seemed to be waging some sort of internal debate. He waited. Finally, she met his gaze evenly.

"Okay, this has nothing to do with why I came back, but you might as well know that I've been married," she said slowly. "Twice."

The announcement shook Wade more than anything else she might have said. The thought of her with any other man was enough to make him want to break things. The idea that she'd cared enough about two men to actually marry them made him a little crazy. He didn't know what to say. What kind of woman had been through two marriages before she turned thirty?

She feigned a halfhearted smile. "You don't have a quick comeback for that, do you?"

He shook his head. "I guess I'm surprised. You don't seem like the kind of woman who'd take a decision about marriage lightly."

"I didn't," she said. "Both times, I thought it was true love. It didn't take long to figure out I was wrong."

"How long?"

"Less than a year both times," she admitted with a rueful expression. "That's why I intend to think long and hard before I make that kind of leap again." She looked straight into his eyes. "I might never be ready to try it again."

Her words left him shaken. Not that he'd intended to pop the question tonight, if ever, but it bothered him to realize that she might never be ready to hear it.

"Sounds to me like you're blaming yourself for something that might not have been your fault," he said. "It usually takes two people to make a bad marriage."

"Thank you for saying that, but in both instances it was my mistake. I exercised lousy judgment. Neither man was who I thought he was."

"Don't you suppose they set out to make you believe they were whatever you wanted them to be? In other words, that they might have deliberately deceived you?" Pretty much the way Travis had deceived his mother.

Lauren seemed completely startled by his understanding of that. "Of course they did," she said at once. "But I should have seen through it."

"Are you some kind of mind reader?" he asked.

"No, but—"

He leaned forward and regarded her intently. "Look, everybody sees what they want to see when they look at another person, especially once their hormones have kicked in. And some people happen to be masters at knowing just which buttons to push. You got taken in. It's not a character flaw. You were just too trusting."

A nasty thought occurred to him. "You're not still pining away for either of those guys, are you?"

She laughed at that, and his mood brightened considerably.

"No way," she said fervently. "That part of my life was over long before I made the decision to come back here."

Satisfaction washed over him. "Good. Then we're both agreed, the past is over with, right? We're looking forward from here on."

Lauren lifted her glass, then tapped it against his bottle of beer. "To the future," she said.

Wade took a long swallow of beer, then echoed, "To the future."

It was suddenly looking brighter than it had in a very long time.

Chapter Eight

Wade stood on the back steps to the main house, frozen in place as Lauren's heated words carried outside. All of his complacency about the future was being destroyed by the half of the argument he could hear.

"Jason, you can forget about it," Lauren snapped in a furious tone Wade had never heard her use. "I've told you at least a hundred times that I am not coming back. Why can't you get it through your head that that part of my life is over?"

Those were the same words she'd spoken to him the night before, but they sounded very different now. Wade's gut churned as he waited to see what would come next.

"No," she said flatly. "No, absolutely not. Look, it was a great run while it lasted, but that's it. No more."

So, he thought, listening to her, despite her claims the night before, she had left someone behind, someone who hadn't liked being dumped, someone who was still pestering her. She had lied to him about the men she'd married. They weren't out of her life, the way she'd insisted. Was it possible that one of them was stalking her? That he hadn't gotten over the divorce? Or could this be someone entirely different, not an ex-husband but a third man who had a hold on her heart—or thought he did?

Just let him show up in Winding River, Wade thought, filled with rage. He'd put an end to any lingering possessiveness this Jason felt toward Lauren. The thought of another man putting his hands on her— having the *right* to put his hands on her—made Wade crazy. And the fact that it did made him crazier yet.

He sucked in a deep breath and tried to calm down. He had no right to let it make him nuts. He knew that. But that didn't seem to ease the tightening in his belly or the raw fury that bubbled up inside. He spun away from the door and headed for the barn. Halfway there, he muttered an oath and turned back.

They had business to discuss. They had made a vow in his kitchen the night before to leave the past alone. He wasn't going to start the day by letting whatever had gone on in Lauren's past get in the way of the here and now, at least not when it came to the horses. When it concerned the two of them…well, that was a whole other issue. One of these days, he'd ask all the questions that were suddenly nagging at him about whether she'd been totally honest about being rid of emotional ties to her ex-husbands or any other man.

By the time he got back to the house, it was quiet. Apparently the call had ended. He rapped on the door and stepped inside, forcing what he hoped was a completely neutral mask onto his face.

He spotted Lauren at once, sitting at the table, her shoulders hunched, her head resting on her arms. Everything about her looked dejected. Wade had never seen her like that before. She reminded him of Miss Molly. Who the hell was this guy who was capable of sapping the fire right out of her?

"Problems?" he asked cautiously, not sure he wanted to provide a sounding board for whatever personal issues she might have that involved another man. It was one thing to hear about past loves in the abstract, but to hear all the telling details might be more than he could stomach.

Her head snapped up at once. "No," she said flatly. "Nothing I can't handle anyway. Did you need me?"

"Grady wanted the two of us to ride over to the Grigsby place today. Grigsby's got a couple of horses for sale. Word is that he might be planning to sell out."

A hint of sadness passed across her face. "I remember Otis Grigsby. Gosh, he must be ninety by now. I'm amazed he's kept that place going as long as he has."

"Grady seems to think it's gone downhill a lot the last couple of years, but he says the one thing the old man would never slack off on was caring for his stock." He studied Lauren's lackluster expression. "Do you feel like coming, or should I head on over alone?"

"Of course I'll come," she said, though without much enthusiasm. "Let me splash some water on my face first. I'll meet you at the truck. Are you taking a trailer along just in case?"

Wade nodded. "Might as well be prepared. The way I hear it, now that Grigsby has made up his mind to go, he's in a hurry."

"Or maybe his son is," Lauren said. "Otis Junior

never did have much patience where his daddy was concerned. I heard he moved to Phoenix years ago. Maybe he's intent on getting his father down there, so caring for him will be less inconvenient.''

''Maybe so. Grady didn't say.'' Wade's gaze narrowed when she showed no sign of moving. Finally, because he couldn't bear to see her looking like this, he dragged out a chair and sat down opposite her. ''Okay, what's going on? And don't tell me it's nothing. You look as if you lost your best friend.''

She met his gaze. ''Sorry. I'm just having a bad morning.'' She shoved her chair back and started to stand.

''Sit,'' Wade ordered. ''Talk to me.''

A flash of fire lit her eyes for an instant, and he thought he might have stirred her temper back to life, but then she sighed and sat back down.

Though he'd vowed to say nothing about what he'd overheard, he couldn't help himself. ''Lauren, dammit, what does this mood of yours have to do with that phone call you were on a few minutes ago?'' he demanded. ''Did you have a little lovers' tiff?''

Bright patches of color darkened her cheeks at that. ''You were listening?'' she asked, practically quivering with indignation.

''It was hard not to. I came to the door and you were shouting at the top of your lungs.''

''So you just stood there and eavesdropped?''

''No, dammit, I walked away.''

Her gaze narrowed. ''You did?''

''What the hell difference does it make whether I did or I didn't? Unless, of course, this lover is still very much in the picture after all. Was it one of your ex-husbands?''

She started to respond, then snapped her mouth shut, her expression vaguely guilty.

"What?" he prodded. "Who is Jason?"

She hesitated for a full minute before responding. "Someone I knew in California," she said eventually, then added pointedly, "Not one of the men I married."

"A lover?" Wade demanded again.

She looked as if she might take offense, but eventually she shook her head. "No. He was a business associate. Nothing more."

Wade wasn't buying it. Nobody had that kind of passionate exchange with a business associate, especially a *former* business associate.

"And that's all you intend to tell me?"

She nodded. "Believe me, Jason doesn't matter. Not anymore."

Wade should have been relieved, but instead he was irritated by her refusal to open up any further. He also found her easy dismissal of the man annoying. Would she dismiss him that cavalierly when their relationship ended? Come to think of it, was her relationship with this Jason even ended? Despite what she claimed, it certainly had sounded as if the two of them had unfinished business. He lost patience with trying to figure it out when it was evident she wasn't going to give him anything further to go on.

"Fine, whatever," he snapped, and stood up. "I'll be waiting in the truck. Don't take too long. We've already wasted enough time this morning."

He turned his back and stalked outside, barely resisting the urge to grab the nearest object and hurl it across the yard. Why did he let her get to him? Why the hell did it matter to him who she'd been with or what secrets she was still keeping from him? She was with him now. Well, at least he had reason to believe they would be together one of these days…unless, of course, she drove him completely nuts in the meantime.

Where the heck did Wade get off cross-examining her like a jealous lover? Lauren was still muttering under her breath as she took her own sweet time about getting ready to ride with him to the Grigsby ranch.

Of course, she might not have been half as upset if she hadn't panicked that he might have overheard something that would give away the secret of her identity. Nothing he'd said, however, suggested that had happened. He was only irritated because she wouldn't tell him what Jason really meant to her. As if that persistent little weasel could mean anything at all.

Her hotshot agent still hadn't given up on that big movie deal. He refused to believe that she had no intention of returning to Hollywood. He couldn't imagine anyone giving up the life she'd had out there to stick around a small town in Wyoming and work with horses. Sometimes Lauren didn't believe it herself. But the bottom line was that she was happier than she had been in years, and Wade Owens was a big part of that…even if in his own way he was almost as infuriating as Jason.

Maybe she should just tell Wade everything and get it over with, she thought as she splashed water on her overheated face. She wasn't that great at being secretive. It was taking a toll on her.

But glancing in the mirror at her reflection, Lauren could see on her own features the fear that the prospect stirred in her. Not only was she not ready to give up her prized anonymity, but given all of Wade's issues with the wealthy, he might walk away the minute he discovered she had oodles and oodles of money in the bank. She needed more time to convince him that none of that mattered, that she was simply a woman who loved horses and ranching as much as he did.

When she finally joined him in the truck, she turned to face him. "I want to make a pact."

He studied her with a guarded expression. "Oh?"

"No more talk about Jason or my ex-husbands or your father. Agreed?"

"How did my father get into that mix?"

"They're all touchy subjects."

"Okay, then. Are we talking today or forever?"

"We'll start with today and see how it goes."

He nodded. "Fair enough, as long as I can say one last thing."

"Go ahead," she said.

"Promise me that if you ever need any help, you'll come to me."

"Help?"

"With this Jason," he said tightly. "If the guy doesn't get your message, let me rephrase it for him."

He sounded so worried, so completely sincere about his desire to protect her, that she leaned across the gear-shift and planted a kiss squarely on his mouth, lingering just long enough to feel the heat flare. When she pulled away, he stared at her, bemused.

"What was that for?" he asked.

"For wanting to fight my battles for me. Not that I'd ever let you, but it's sweet just the same."

"I didn't offer to be 'sweet,'" he grumbled.

"I know, that's why it was so wonderful. Now let's get over to see Mr. Grigsby. I feel like doing some high-powered horse-trading."

Wade laughed, the last of his tension draining out of

his face. "Good. Then I'll let you negotiate. The man will be so dazzled, he's bound to give us rock-bottom prices."

"Very funny. I will not use my looks to get a better deal."

"Too bad. I'm here to tell you it's your best weapon."

"Then you haven't heard me sweet-talking anyone yet," she assured him with a grin.

His grin spread. "I can hardly wait."

"You should have heard Lauren," Wade boasted to Grady when they returned to the Blackhawk ranch with four magnificent horses, all bought at prices well below market value. "She was amazing."

"I just did a little negotiating," Lauren insisted. "Otis Junior was anxious to sell, and I took advantage of that."

"Otis Junior was tongue-tied and all but on his knees by the time you finished with him," Wade corrected. "I've never seen anything like it. I'm just glad you were on our side."

He realized then that Karen and Grady were exchanging a thoroughly amused, knowing look. "Of course, you two know she's good. You've probably seen her in action. This was a first for me. I've never before known anyone who could rob a man blind and make him grateful for it."

"Thank you, I think," Lauren said.

"Trust me, it was a compliment, darlin'. I would have kissed you on the spot, but I was afraid it might shake the delicate balance of the negotiations. I think Otis Junior will be calling before the night's over to ask you out himself."

"Otis Junior is a pig," she said, dismissing the man. "He has a wife and four children down in Phoenix and everyone knows it."

"That didn't seem to stop him from thinking he'd made a conquest this afternoon," Wade said. In fact, for a minute, he'd almost belted the man for daring to look at Lauren as if she were high-priced beef available for the right price. Then he'd realized that Lauren was in total control of the situation, and he'd forced himself to sit back and let her run with it.

"All part of the strategy," she assured him now.

"I want to hear everything," Karen said. "Dinner's in the oven. We're expecting you two to join us."

"I've got to get the horses settled," Wade argued.

"And I need to help him," Lauren said.

"And dinner will wait till you're done," Karen said. "You're not getting out of this, so hurry before the pot roast overcooks."

Wade resigned himself to an evening of probing questions and pointed looks. He knew that Grady and Karen had a whole lot of ideas about him and Lauren. He shared quite a few of them, but that didn't mean he wanted to have his every action held under a microscope.

"It's going to be a long evening," Lauren noted as they unloaded the horses from the trailer and led them into the barn.

"Yeah, I got that impression," he said.

"You could get out of it," she offered. "There's no reason both of us need to be cross-examined."

Wade paused in what he was doing and met her gaze. "Here's the thing. The way I see it, we're in this together." He grinned. "Besides, if we're both there when they're poking and prodding, there's less likelihood we'll get our stories mixed up.''

Lauren laughed. "I see you've caught on to their divide-and-conquer strategy.''

He nodded. "Not five minutes after you showed up," he said. "There was no mistaking which way the wind was blowing with those two. They've been hoping something will happen between us."

"You don't mind?"

"Not if you don't."

"Oddly enough, I don't. Normally I'd hate the meddling, but it's Karen and Grady." She chuckled. "Besides, I gave them fits when they were seeing each other. I guess they have a right to bug me. I'm surprised you're not bothered by it, though. It pretty much puts you on the spot."

"I'm only on the spot if I want to be there," he said, and met her gaze evenly. "There's no point in denying the obvious. We've got a lot of chemistry between us. We might not know what we're going to do about it yet, but that won't make it go away. And they're not going to be able to rush us into anything that both of us aren't ready for. Agreed?"

"Agreed," she said solemnly, and held out her hand.

Wade grinned. "I think a pact like that deserves more than a handshake, don't you?"

Gaze clashing with hers, he crossed the barn and tucked a finger under her chin. Slowly, he lowered his head until their lips met. The solemnity of the gesture pretty much got lost in the explosion of need that rocked through both of them. He had to drag himself away before he tossed her down on the hay and took them right back to the edge of passion they'd reached the day before. One of these days there would be no turning back, but not tonight.

"I think we'd better get to dinner while I can still walk," he said wryly.

"It's possible you'll have to carry me," she said, her own expression rueful. "I think you made my knees too weak to hold me up."

"Gladly," he said, and scooped her into his arms until she was cradled against his chest. Unfortunately, that put her tempting mouth within inches of his own.

"Bad idea," he said, and lowered her to her feet. "I think you're going to have to get there under your own steam."

"Too bad. I kind of liked your way."

"Me, too, but my way was likely to land us in a heap of trouble," he said with regret. "I'm pretty certain neither of us wants Grady and Karen to wonder what's taking us so long and come looking, especially if they're likely to find us making love in a pile of hay."

"Oh, I don't know," she said, giving him a wink over her shoulder as she sashayed past. "At least it would put an end to all that wild speculating they're doing up at the house right now."

Two nights later, Lauren sat at a table at Stella's and endured a whole host of speculative looks from the Calamity Janes. Apparently Karen had been busy sharing information with the others about the budding romance out at the Blackhawk ranch.

"But what do we really know about this guy?" Emma demanded. "I think we need to look into his background."

Lauren frowned. "He's a wrangler. Grady interviewed him. He's excellent at what he does. Isn't that enough? You met him. Does he strike you as anything other than a decent, hardworking cowboy?''

Emma waved off the question. "First impressions don't count. I'd feel better if we knew more. For all we know he could be after your money.''

"He doesn't know I have any," Lauren said quietly. The others stared at her.

"How can that be?" Gina asked. "He has to know you're a Hollywood superstar.''

Lauren shook her head. Karen chimed in to confirm it. "He doesn't even know her last name. We sort of made sure it never came up.''

"That's what you *think*," Emma insisted. "It's entirely possible he's known all along. Even out here in the wilds of Wyoming, Lauren has made a name for herself. Surely he's seen her face on a supermarket tabloid or on some TV talk show.''

Again, Lauren shook her head. "I don't think so. He has issues with rich people. If he knew who I am and what my net worth is, he'd run the other way.''

"Not likely," Cassie scoffed. "What man would turn his back on that? I'm with Emma. I think we need to be sure he's not a golddigger.''

Lauren frowned. "Did I put your men on the spot like that?''

"Yes," they replied in a chorus.

"I did not," she insisted, then shrugged. "Okay, maybe I gave some of them a rough time to make sure they weren't out to hurt you, but I didn't go snooping around trying to get dirt on them.''

"Gee, that wasn't how it seemed to Rafe when you confronted him with his society page mentions from the New York papers," Gina teased. "The ones you researched on the Internet within ten minutes of meeting him.''

''I was just being protective,'' Lauren said, undaunted.

''And that's what we're being now,'' Emma told her. ''I can call an investigator and have him do a quick check just to be sure there are no major skeletons rattling around in Wade's closet.''

''Absolutely not,'' Lauren said, horrified by the idea. ''I will never speak to you again if you do that. I know everything I need to know about Wade Owens.''

''Sweetie, I have just two words for you,'' Emma said. *''Two divorces.''*

Lauren groaned. ''Okay, my judgment was impaired, but I've learned my lesson. Besides, I have Grady and Karen to back me up. They like Wade.'' She turned to Karen. ''Right?''

Karen nodded. ''I don't think Grady would have him working at the ranch—much less be encouraging a relationship with Lauren—if he didn't have total faith in Wade's honesty.''

''Maybe so,'' Emma began.

''That's it,'' Lauren said, cutting her off. ''No investigator.''

Emma sighed. ''Okay, I'll agree to that on one condition.''

Lauren regarded her with suspicion. ''Which is?''

''We all get to spend time with him,'' she replied. ''Check him out. See how he fits in with the Calamity Janes and our guys.''

Cassie's eyes lit up. ''Perfect. A party is just what we need. We can have it at our place. Cole needs to learn how to fire up that humongous gas grill he insisted he had to have.''

"He can cook the steaks, but I'm bringing everything else," Gina said, jumping on the bandwagon. "Everybody have their calendars? I want to be sure Rafe's going to be in town. We never get to do anything fun together." As soon as the words left her mouth, she blushed furiously. "Well, nothing in public anyway."

Lauren laughed. "Then this will definitely be good practice for your social skills."

Only Karen looked worried by the plan. "Are you sure Wade will go along with this, especially if it's at Cassie's?"

"Why wouldn't he? He's in here all the time. He knows me," Cassie said.

"Yes," Karen agreed. "But he probably doesn't know that you're married to one of the richest computer geniuses in the universe. Once he gets a load of that house you and Cole built, he's going to conclude you don't need the tips."

Cassie grinned. "I don't. I have the most overloaded piggy bank in ten states. All that money is going to end up in a trust fund for the kids."

"Which brings up another point," Lauren said. "Why are you still working here? I thought after the baby came, you'd give up the job."

"Never. It's what I do," Cassie said simply. "Just like you want to work with horses, even though your glamorous Hollywood career left you rich enough to retire. I like being with people, finding out what's going on around town. It gives structure to my days. I'd go nuts sitting around the house while Cole shuts himself away with his mysterious computer software. Besides, I don't put in that many hours. I have plenty of time for the baby and Jake."

"Good point," Gina said. "We're all independent women. We love our men, but we want more." She lifted her soft drink. "To us and the lucky men who have us."

"Amen," Emma said as they clinked their glasses together.

"So, are we agreed? I'll have the party at my place?" Cassie asked.

Lauren hesitated, giving Karen's concern a little more consideration, then nodded. "I think it'll be good for Wade to see that people aren't automatically bad just because they have money. He's already excused Grady and Karen from his generalization. If I can get him to look beyond the dollars with a few more people, maybe I can finally tell him exactly what I did for a living over the last ten years."

"We could always let it slip out at the party," Emma said. "Watch his reaction. Then we'd know for sure whether he's known all along."

"I predict that finding out he's been sleeping with a superstar is going to be quite a shock," Gina said. "I don't think a party with Lauren's friends is the place for that particular revelation."

Lauren blushed. "I agree. Besides, he hasn't exactly been sleeping with me," she said, then grinned. "Not yet, anyway, but I have high hopes for tonight."

"Tonight?" they chorused, glancing pointedly at the clock above the counter. It was already eight-thirty.

"I figure his defenses will be weak at this hour," she said, then lifted the package beside her. "Besides, the sexy new nightie I ordered just came in. It's guaranteed to make him forget why sleeping with me is a bad idea." Never mind that she had been the one holding out till the time was right. This would send Wade the message loud and clear that that time was now. She was counting on extraordinary sex to make the news of her identity—and the fact that she'd deliberately kept it from him—a bit more palatable to Wade.

"Let me see," Gina insisted, peeking into the box at the scraps of pale peach lace. "Oh, my," she whispered, fanning herself. "And Rafe's in New York."

She passed on the package.

"But Cole isn't," Cassie said, scooting out of the booth as soon as she'd caught a glimpse of the gown.

"Grady, either," Karen added, right behind her.

"And, lucky me, Ford is right across the street," Emma noted. She looked at Lauren. "Are you sure you're not going to be wasting this on Wade? I'd pay big bucks to take it off your hands."

Lauren snatched the package away from her. "Get your own."

"In Winding River?" Emma asked.

"I'll bring you the catalog," Lauren promised. "I have big plans for this one."

And if Wade didn't cooperate, she was going to have to reconsider whether he was half as smart as she'd given him credit for being.

Chapter Nine

Wade had been restless all evening long. He'd gone up to the house earlier and discovered that both Lauren and Karen had gone into town to get together with their friends. Grady was taking the opportunity to catch up on ranch paperwork, but Wade was at loose ends. For the first time in years, he didn't like having time on his hands.

He'd sat on his front porch for an hour, truck keys in hand, considering a trip into Winding River for a drink at the Heartbreak. In the end, he'd just gone inside, gotten a beer from the fridge and popped the top. He'd drunk that one and two more on the porch, trying not to admit to himself that he was watching the driveway for the return of Karen Blackhawk's car.

When the headlights finally cut through the inky darkness, something that felt an awful lot like relief eased through him. He knew then that he was a goner when it came to Lauren.

The car came to a stop close to the main house, and feminine laughter drifted on the night air. He was able to separate Lauren's low-pitched laugh from Karen's with no trouble at all. It was the one that sent a shiver down his spine.

He had two choices. He could sit right here, satisfied with the knowledge that she was home safely. Or he could drum up a flimsy excuse and go on over to the house so he could catch a glimpse of her before she went off to bed. So what if she figured out that he'd been watching for her? He was past the point of trying to hide his desire for her, wasn't he?

Before he could decide whether to follow his usual cautious route or risk making an idiot out of himself, he heard a whisper of sound. Searching the shadows, he spotted Lauren heading his way. So, he thought with satisfaction, that settled that. She was coming to him. It remained to be seen precisely what that meant.

"Is there any more of that wine from the other night?" she asked as she stepped onto the porch.

He nodded and stood up. "The rest of the bottle's in the fridge. I'll get you a glass." He eyed the package she was carrying. "What's that?"

A wicked grin flitted across her face. "You'll see," she said. "Why don't I get the wine? You need another beer?"

He sat back down and lifted his half-full bottle. "Nope. I'm good."

"I'll say," she murmured as she slipped past him, her perfume every bit as taunting as her words.

Gaze narrowed, he watched her go inside. The woman was up to something, no doubt about it. And

it had something to do with that package she was carrying. The prospect of discovering exactly what she
was up to filled him with an edgy sense of anticipation.

When she hadn't returned within the couple of
minutes it would take to pour a glass of wine, Wade
grew increasingly suspicious. Eventually he heard a
rustle of sound and turned toward the door. Lust
promptly slammed through him like a freight train.

"What in the name of all that's holy…?" he murmured before his mouth went dry.

Lauren stood framed in the doorway, wearing something…well, he assumed it qualified as something…what there was of it. Every pale curve, even the
dusky peaks of her breasts were plainly visible through
the sheer peach fabric that dipped to a low V in front
and barely skimmed the tops of her thighs. He'd imagined those creamy, shapely thighs in his dreams, but it
turned out his imagination hadn't been nearly vivid
enough to capture the sensuous reality.

As for the rest, the subtly rounded hips, the generous
breasts…they were every man's fantasy. He was hard
as a rock, and so hot, he felt as if the sun were blazing
down instead of a pale moon. He had to resist the need
to wipe the sudden perspiration from his brow.

"Well?" Lauren whispered, her expression expectant.

He struggled to find words, struggled even harder to
prevent himself from snatching her into his arms and
hauling her straight to his bed.

"I'm speechless," he managed to say finally in a
choked voice.

She gave him a coy look. "Speechless in a good
way, I hope."

"Do you honestly need to ask?"

"Since you haven't budged, yes, I think I do."

"It's better this way," he said. "If I get out of this chair, there's no telling what I might do."

"That's the idea."

Again, he swallowed hard and fought temptation. "Not until I know what brought this on."

"You've said it yourself," she said. "We've been heading down this road since the day we met. I've just decided it's time to see what's at the end of the road."

"But why now? Why tonight? What the hell went on while you were in town?"

She shrugged and one skinny little strap of the gown slid down her shoulder, allowing even more flesh to be exposed. She ignored it, but Wade couldn't seem to tear his gaze away. He was way past the point of resisting, but at least he could make a pretense of a valiant struggle. Suddenly that seemed to be a point of honor, to demonstrate a little self-control rather than stripping that scrap of material right off her.

Lauren opened the screen door and stepped onto the porch. Wade cast a frantic look toward the main house, praying that neither Grady nor Karen had the same clear, backlit view he was getting. He bolted to his feet.

"Maybe we should go inside," he said, getting between her and the main house to block any view.

Her lips curved up in the smile of a pure seductress who knew she'd won the battle. Not even a saint could have resisted that smile. "For a minute there, you had me worried," she said as she stepped back across the threshold.

"I doubt that," he muttered. "You've had this under control from the minute you got here."

Inside, even with only one lamp lit, he could still see the satisfaction in her eyes at his words. He dared a step closer, so that he could risk a touch to see if she was as warm and inviting as she appeared. It was like touching a flame, far more dangerous to him than to her.

"You still haven't answered my question," he noted.

Her gaze locked with his. "Which was?"

"Why now?"

"It seemed like the right time. If we waited any longer, we'd just end up analyzing it to death. I'm a big believer in spontaneity."

"So you decided on action," he concluded, finally permitting himself a full-fledged grin.

"Do you object?"

Wade was surprised by the hint of vulnerability behind her words. How could she not know that she took his breath away, that he wanted her so much he physically ached from it?

"Not a chance," he assured her, lowering his mouth to cover hers.

This time there was no holding back. They both knew the kiss was a prelude to more. Much more. Wade took his time with it, tasting, savoring, even as he deliberately kept his hands off her. Once he felt that heated skin again, once his caresses began to roam with nothing but filmy material between him and her exquisite body, the fire would rage out of control in no time. Better to take things slowly, to concentrate on making this kiss so memorable neither of them would ever forget it.

Just the kiss.

For now.

Time stood still. It was amazing, he thought when he could think at all, how many nuances there were to a kiss. Dark and dangerous. Sweet and heady. Languid, lazy matings of tongue and teeth. Dizzying, breath-stealing brandings. Quick, tantalizing pecks. They tried them all. No one was better than the others. They were all mind-numbingly spectacular. Cumulatively, they made his heart pound and his blood roar.

Lauren made soft little whimpers of sound deep in her throat that drove him crazy. When she swayed toward him, he caught her, his fingers skimming silky skin and slippery, felt-like-nothing fabric. Restraint flew out the window.

His hands were everywhere then, exploring curves, searching for secret heat and moistness, turning her quiet moans to shuddering demands. She was the most giving lover he'd ever met, opening herself eagerly to him, sharing her pleasure with delight, taunting him with desperate touches of her own that shook him to his very core.

And here they were, still in the living room, still on their feet, though Lauren had sagged against him in weak-kneed surrender more than once. He held her steady and gazed into her eyes.

"I guess we're not going to call it quits this time, are we?" he asked seriously, his gaze searching hers.

"If you do, I'd have to kill you," she said with such fervent desperation that it made him grin.

"We can't have that," he said, scooping her into his arms and heading for the house's tiny bedroom, grateful that for once he'd done more than haphazardly toss the bedspread over the tangled sheets before he left in the morning.

There wasn't much to the room—a double bed, a pine dresser, an overstuffed chair beside an ancient floor lamp, impersonal furnishings for a room that had

had its share of occupants through the years. It suited him just fine, but it was hardly the romantic setting the impending event deserved. It would have to do, he thought as he crossed the threshold and gently placed Lauren on the bed.

She looked like a temptress or a mythical goddess against the dark blue bedspread, her red hair spilled across the pillow. The filmy, barely there fabric of her gown was more temptation than covering for a body made for loving.

And she was his, all his, Wade thought with a sense of awe as he stripped off his clothes and joined her.

The heat between them was fanned alive by his first touch, then escalated by hers until there was nothing between them but need and urgency and demanding pleas. He slid off the scraps of lace, tossed them aside and watched, mesmerized, as the gown floated to the floor.

But then the only thing mesmerizing him was Lauren, her gaze dark with desire as he knelt above her, her perfect bow of a mouth parted with a sigh of fulfillment as he slowly slid into her.

This, he thought as the tight, velvet moistness surrounded him, must be what all the books were written about. Not the hasty unions he'd enjoyed in the past, but this sweet mating that began with the quick flame of kindling, built into something urgent and then exploded into a conflagration that could wipe out thoughts and consume a man.

He covered Lauren's mouth with his to capture a scream just as her body shuddered with a violent release that triggered his own. Clinging together, they let the waves of pleasure ebb slowly.

Reluctant to let it end, Wade stayed where he was until he could feel himself growing hard again inside her, the urgency every bit as powerful as the first time, the release—when it finally came—every bit as satisfying. The amazement and delight in Lauren's eyes was as rewarding as any gift he'd ever received.

He rolled onto his back, carrying her with him, then gazed into her eyes and grinned. "I think you did it anyway," he murmured.

"Did what?" she asked.

"Killed me."

She tweaked a hair on his chest, drawing a sharp response. "Nope," she said happily. "Still alive."

"How reassuring," he said wryly. "You must be awfully satisfied with yourself, coming over here tonight and having your way with me."

She regarded him with an innocent expression that she managed to make look surprisingly sincere. "Is that how you think it happened?"

"I know it is."

"Are you complaining?"

"Even if I had any breath to spare, I wouldn't complain," he assured her. "You were everything I imagined and then some."

"Does that mean we can keep doing this?"

Try to stop it, he thought. "I don't see why not," he said, careful as he tried to gauge her mood. It seemed a little edgy, a little unpredictable.

"Now?" she inquired.

Wade feigned a moan.

"Are you turning me down?" she asked, wiggling against him.

He laughed as his body responded. "Guess not."

Satisfied with a job very well done, Lauren showered and scooted down to the barn before dawn. She was coaxing Midnight out into the corral by the time Wade sauntered down a half hour later with a mug of coffee in hand.

"You were up early," he noted as he handed her the coffee.

"I figured if I didn't get out of there before you woke up, there was a very good chance neither one of us would get to work today."

"Grady does owe me a few days off," he said, giving her a deliberately suggestive once-over. "Today could have been one of them."

"I would love to have heard that call," she teased him, feeling amazingly comfortable with their new-found intimacy.

"There's still time. I can make it now and we can be back in bed in five minutes."

Lauren shook her head. "Afraid not. I have a date with another male." When Wade's expression immediately darkened, she gestured toward Midnight. "Don't tell me you're jealous of a horse."

He shrugged ruefully. "Could be," he said. "Don't test me."

She patted his cheek. "You'll get over it, once you realize I'm all yours."

There was an unmistakable flicker of alarm in his eyes. Determined not to let it linger, she quickly added, "As long as all you're after is a quick romp in the hay."

His gaze narrowed. "Is that all you really want, Lauren?"

She forced out the words she knew he wanted to hear. "It's all I really want." *For now,* she amended silently.

* * *

Wade still wasn't sure how he'd let Lauren talk him into going to this party with her. What the hell business did he have socializing with a megabucks computer genius like Cole Davis? Unfortunately, his protests had fallen on deaf ears. One thing he was learning about Lauren was that once she got a notion into her head, there was no talking her out of it. And she wanted to go to this barbecue, seemingly every bit as badly as she'd wanted to finesse her way into his bed the other night.

"Why are you resisting?" she had demanded finally. "Don't you want to be seen with me in public?"

"Don't be ridiculous," Wade had snapped.

"Then it must be because the party is at Cole's," she'd guessed, hitting the nail on the head on the first real try. "Have you even met him?"

"No, we're not likely to travel in the same circles," he'd said wryly.

She'd given him a pitying look. "Is that so? Who serves you dinner at Stella's more often than not?"

He'd stared at her blankly. "Are you talking about Cassie?"

She'd nodded. "Cassie *Davis,* Cole's wife."

Wade had been stunned. "Cassie is married to Cole Davis and she's waiting tables in a diner? You have to be kidding me. What kind of man—"

Lauren had cut him off, grinning. "Don't even go there. It drives Cole crazy, but Cassie loves her job. She pretty much told him he could complain from now till doomsday, but she wasn't giving it up," she said proudly, then studied him with a penetrating look. "Still think you won't fit in at this party? Grady and Karen will be there, too."

"Okay, fine," he'd grumbled, defeated.

Now, as he turned his truck into the long driveway that led up to a sprawling new ranch house, his second thoughts came flooding back. The house had soaring panels of glass and the kind of custom details that could be spotted even from a distance. The home he'd grown up in would have fit in one tiny alcove of this place. Even Grady's spacious house was small by comparison.

Before Wade could get all of his defenses firmly in place, Lauren was tugging him into the middle of a throng of people, introducing him to a group of women she referred to as the Calamity Janes, her best friends from high school. He already knew Cassie and Karen. To his surprise, Gina Petrillo from Tony's Italian restaurant was another of them. And that attorney he'd met at the Blackhawks' one morning, Emma Hamilton, was the fifth.

He realized Lauren was regarding him with amusement. "What?" he asked.

"Feeling better? You already know half the crowd. They're not that scary, are they? Now, let's go for broke and I'll introduce you to the men."

Wade studied the cluster of males around the barbecue with surprise. Looking at them, it was impossible to tell which ones had money and which did not. They were all wearing faded jeans and T-shirts and well-worn boots. If he'd had to hazard a guess, he would have said they were all in the same income bracket he was. All except one, anyway. His jeans actually looked as if they'd been pressed at the dry cleaners and though his shirt was western in style, it was as starched as any dress shirt hanging in Wade's closet. He pegged him right off as the wealthy Cole Davis.

To his astonishment, he was flat-out wrong. Davis was in the same well-worn cowboy attire as the rest of them. The man in the fancier duds was Rafe O'Donnell, Gina's fiancé.

"You'll have to excuse him," Gina said to Wade, tucking her arm through the man's. "Rafe is a bigshot New York lawyer. This is his idea of dressing down. We're working on it. I'm going to take him out to the barn for a romp in the hay before the afternoon is over and try to mess him up a little."

Lauren winked at Wade. "Definitely something for him to look forward to, right, Wade?"

Wade felt a rush of heat to his face. "I don't think they want to hear about that."

"I certainly do," Gina assured him.

"Me, too," Rafe agreed, clearly fascinated.

"Well, my mama taught me it is never polite to kiss and tell, so I'm sorry, but I can't be the one to satisfy your curiosity," Wade said.

"Oh, that's okay," Gina said blithely. "I can get Lauren to blab almost anything."

Wade frowned down at Lauren. "Is that so?"

"Well, not everything," she assured him. "A smart woman always has some secrets."

"Maybe we'd better talk about that," Wade said, steering her away from her friends.

She gazed up at him, her expression innocent. "Something wrong?"

"Just how much of our private business do you share with the universe?"

She stiffened at his curt tone. "I don't share any of it with the universe," she said tightly. "But I do talk to my friends. They care about me. They want to know what's going on in my life, so, yes, they know that I care about you. Is that a problem?''

Wade forced himself to relax. ''And that's all?''

''Why does this make you so uncomfortable?''

Wade didn't have a ready answer for that. Was it because the more her friends knew, the more likely they were to have expectations for his relationship with Lauren? Was he afraid of the pressure? Or was it just his natural inclination for privacy after years of enduring the gossip about being the bastard son of a Montana power broker?

''I don't like the world knowing my business,'' he said finally.

She returned his gaze with an unblinking look. ''Believe me, neither do I, and I probably have more experience with it than you do.''

''I doubt that,'' he retorted. ''Half of Montana thought my mother and I were fair game.''

Lauren's mouth opened, but no words came out. Instead, she merely snapped it shut and walked away, leaving Wade staring after her. Because he was in no mood to continue the conversation either, he grabbed a beer and wandered over toward the corral to take a look at the horses. The next thing he knew, he was joined by a boy who looked to be about ten. Except for his thick-lensed glasses, he was the spitting image of Cole Davis.

''Hi, I'm Jake,'' the boy said. ''Grady says you work with the horses at his place.''

Wade nodded. ''You like horses?''

''Sure. My grandpa taught me to ride when my mom and me moved here a year ago. That was before she and my dad got married.''

''Your dad?''

"Cole Davis," Jake confirmed. "He's probably the smartest guy in the whole world when it comes to computers and stuff. I didn't know him when I was little, but then we came back and he and my mom got married, and it turned out he was my real dad all along."

Wade heard Jake's matter-of-fact recitation with increasing amazement and mounting indignation. It was all too reminiscent of his own situation, even though this one had obviously had a far happier ending. Still, it added fuel to his belief that the rich had their own way of doing things, with little sense of decency figured into the equation.

He would have whirled away, gone after Lauren and insisted on leaving, except Jake was staring up at him with a wide-eyed look, clearly waiting for some sort of response. Wade struggled to come up with something neutral that wouldn't reveal the turmoil his thoughts were in.

"I imagine you were glad to get to know your dad," he said finally.

"You bet," Jake said eagerly. "I already knew all about him, because I read all this computer stuff. When it turned out we were related, it was, like, the best thing ever."

Wade knew he couldn't ask a kid why he hadn't resented the man who'd deserted him years earlier. The situations might not have been as similar as they sounded. Whatever the case, he wasn't sure he could spend five minutes in Cole's company without wanting to slug the guy on the boy's behalf.

And what was wrong with Cassie that she'd turned around and married a man who'd ignored her and their kid for all those years?

Wade forced a smile for Jake's benefit. "Good talking to you. Maybe one of these days you can come by the Blackhawk ranch and show me how well you ride. I can give you some pointers."

Jake's eyes brightened. "Really? That would be so awesome."

"We'll definitely set it up, then." He looked around for Lauren. "I'd better go see what happened to my date."

"Lauren's out back by the pool," Jake said. He looked up at Wade shyly. "She's really, really pretty, isn't she?"

Wade grinned at his awestruck tone. He understood it all too well. "She is, indeed."

"I was hoping maybe she'd marry me when I grow up, but I guess since she's with you, I'd better forget about it," Jake said, then added with a hopeful note, "unless things, maybe, aren't working out for you guys."

"They're working out well enough for now," he told Jake solemnly. "But I'm sure Lauren will be glad to know you're waiting in the wings in case I blow things."

"Oh, gosh, you can't tell her that," Jake pleaded. "It would make me look like such a dumb geek."

Wade ruffled his hair. "Hey, there's nothing dumb about falling for a beautiful woman. No woman can have too many admirers." He winked at him. "And you're never too young to start looking out for the best."

He managed to hide his grin until after he'd walked away. So, he thought, Lauren was making conquests among the elementary-school set. He'd better stake his claim fast.

As promised, he found her out by the pool, wearing

a two-piece bathing suit that almost had his tongue falling out. It took everything in him not to grab a towel—or better yet a blanket, if only one had been handy—and toss it over her.

Instead, he drew a lounge chair up beside her. "Hey, good-looking, I have it on excellent authority that I have competition in this crowd."

She slid her sunglasses down her nose and stared at him over the top. "Oh?"

"Jake is smitten. He says if I blow it, he's waiting in the wings."

"Jake, huh?" She smiled. "He's a very smart boy. He takes after his daddy in that regard."

Wade stiffened. "You and Cole had a thing?"

She frowned at the question. "Don't be ridiculous. He never had eyes for anyone except Cassie."

"Then why the hell did he abandon her and their son?" he blurted before he could stop himself.

Sudden understanding dawned on her face. "Oh, I get it. You're comparing their situation to yours. It wasn't like that," she insisted. "Cole never knew Cassie was pregnant. It's a complicated story, but their parents managed to keep them apart. When Cassie came back to town and Cole found out about Jake, he was furious. He insisted that Cassie marry him so he could be a real father to Jake. It was a pretty tense standoff for a while, but they were meant for each other and everything's perfect now."

She painted such a rosy picture, Wade thought, unable to squelch the bitterness that was always close to the surface when anything reminded him of his own past.

"I'm sorry," Lauren said quietly. "I know hearing

about Cole and Cassie and Jake must bring up a lot of bad memories.''

"Yeah, you could say that." He met her gaze. "Would you mind if we got out of here?"

"Now?" she asked, regarding him with surprise. "We haven't even eaten."

"Suddenly I'm not all that hungry," he said. "If you want to stick around, I'm sure you could hitch a ride back with Karen and Grady."

"No," she said at once, getting to her feet. "If you're leaving, so am I. I'll explain to Cassie." She winked. "I'm sure I can make her understand how anxious we are to be alone."

Not entirely sure whether she was serious, Wade regarded her with alarm, but Lauren reached up and stroked his cheek.

"I'll tell her I have a headache," she reassured him.

"Thanks."

Her gaze captured his and held. "But I'm pretty sure I'll be miraculously cured by the time we get home if you want to make it up to me for tearing me away from my friends."

Despite his sour mood, Wade chuckled. "I definitely think we can work something out."

"Then what are you waiting for? Get that truck started," she said.

She said it with an eagerness that made his heart flip over. Somehow in the last couple of months, he'd gotten lucky. Experience had taught him that luck seldom lasted, but he was going to ride this streak for as long as he possibly could.

Chapter Ten

The barbecue at Cole's had been a bad idea. Lauren could see that now. It had just reminded Wade of everything he was bitter about in his own life. Even though the circumstances were entirely different, she could see why hearing about Cole and Jake had just reconfirmed for him that wealthy, powerful men took whatever they wanted and to hell with everyone else.

Though it bothered her that Wade hadn't been willing to stay and get to know Cole, even after she had explained that he wasn't to blame for abandoning Cassie, she had been more than willing to go home and spend the afternoon in his arms.

Still, it had been a wake-up call, reminding her that Wade wasn't going to take the news of her own economic situation in stride the way she'd hoped he might. Even though it was increasingly evident how he felt about her, she didn't doubt for a second that could change in a heartbeat if he discovered she'd been deliberately deceiving him all this time. And that didn't even take into account the whole superstar thing.

"'Oh, what a tangled web we weave, when first we practice to deceive,'" she muttered as she brushed down Midnight. The horse whinnied in apparent agreement.

In the last week, he'd been more and more docile, accepting her touch, allowing her to groom him without the slightest hint of trepidation. These sessions were less about the grooming itself and more about getting Midnight used to being handled. She had a feeling that in another week or so she could try putting a saddle on him. Grady and Wade were both pleased with the stallion's progress, though they were anxious for the day when he could become the magnificent stud they'd envisioned when they'd bought him.

Miss Molly was another story entirely. Nothing Lauren had tried made an iota of difference in the horse's demeanor. She was losing weight, and her coat was losing its luster.

As soon as Lauren finished with Midnight, she turned him out to pasture, then went back for Miss Molly. She led the filly into the corral just as Emma pulled into the yard. Caitlyn tumbled out of the car, clutching something in her arms.

Lauren climbed over the paddock fence and walked over to meet them. Caitlyn raced up to her, her face alight with excitement.

"Aunt Lauren, guess what? Remember I told you that my cat had kittens? This is one of them." She all but shoved the squirming little ball of fluff into Lauren's hands. "Isn't she cute?"

The black-and-white kitten had huge green eyes,

which regarded Karen with a solemn stare. Then she
yawned widely and let out a plaintive meow.

To Lauren's astonishment, there was a slight whinny
of acknowledgment from the paddock. She turned
around to discover that Miss Molly's ears were pricked
up. When the cat meowed again, the horse edged
closer, practically shoving her head into Lauren's
shoulder as if to get a better look.

"Well, well, well," Lauren said, a grin spreading
across her face as she took the kitten from Caitlyn and
held her a bit closer to the horse. The kitten was purr-
ing like a little engine. "Is this what's been missing
from your life, Miss Molly? Did you have a barn cat
at the old ranch?"

As if to confirm it, Miss Molly's tongue swiped the
kitten, which promptly shook itself and hissed at her.
Clearly not a match made in heaven, Lauren thought.
Still, she thought she knew now what it would take to
get Wade's horse back to her old self.

"Do you have plans for this kitten?" she asked Caitlyn.

"No, she most certainly does not," Emma said emphatically. "You want her, she's yours."

Lauren ignored Emma and kept her gaze on Caitlyn.
"Are you sure you don't mind?"

Caitlyn frowned. "I guess not. Mom said I had to
get rid of one of them anyway. How come you want
her?"

"I think Miss Molly here needs a friend," Lauren
explained.

"A horse wants to be friends with a kitten?" Caitlyn
asked, clearly fascinated by the idea. "Won't she hurt
the kitten?"

"I'll see that she doesn't," Lauren promised. "Until

she's bigger and until she and Miss Molly are used to each other, I'll keep her in the office except when I'm around. So, what do you think? Is it a deal?''

Emma nudged her daughter. "Say yes."

"Okay, okay," Caitlyn said. "But I can come see her, right?"

"Anytime you want. Have you named her yet?"

Caitlyn shook her head. "Mom said it would be harder to give her up if she had a name."

Lauren grinned at Emma. "Your mom is a very smart woman. What would you think if we called her Good Golly?"

"That's a funny name," Caitlyn said, her nose wrinkled as she considered it.

Emma chuckled. "I get it." She looked at her daughter. "There was a very popular song way back in the fifties, 'Good Golly, Miss Molly.' ''

"Then together they'd have the name of the song," Caitlyn concluded. "Cool."

"Definitely cool," Lauren agreed. She could hardly wait to share the news with Wade.

Something was up with Lauren. She'd been casting strange looks his way all through dinner. Wade couldn't get a grip on what was going on. When he asked, she just mumbled some nonsense about having had a great day and refused to say another word.

But as soon as dinner was over and the dishes were cleared away, she announced casually, "I think I'll take a walk down to the barn. Want to come along, Wade?"

"I spent all day on a horse. Why would I want to go see more of them?" he grumbled.

"Trust me," she said with a suggestive wink. "I'll make it worth your while."

His lack of enthusiasm vanished in a heartbeat. "Now that's an invitation a man would have to be insane to turn down," he said, and followed her outside.

It was a hot, still night with no evidence that it was likely to cool down. Wade would have been perfectly happy to sit in a rocker on the porch, Lauren in his lap, and try to stir up a breeze.

Instead, they were kicking up dust and getting overheated in a far less interesting way. Still, maybe that payoff she'd promised at the barn would be worth it. In fact, he was counting on it.

It was cooler inside the shadowy depths of the barn. Lauren paused first at Midnight's stall, offered the horse a cube of sugar and filled Wade in on his progress. The matter-of-fact recitation suggested this wasn't why they'd come.

Before they moved off toward Miss Molly's stall, Lauren stopped him. "Wait here. I have to get something."

Wade had visions of a blanket, maybe a couple of ice-cold beers, a handful of juicy strawberries. When Lauren came back with none of those things, he barely restrained a sigh of disappointment. He regarded the flannel shirt she was carrying—one of his, if he wasn't mistaken—with suspicion.

"What do you have there?"

"You'll see," she said, once again giving him that mysterious smile.

She led the way to Miss Molly's stall. To his astonishment, the horse immediately perked up as they neared.

"What the devil...?" he murmured. "How did this happen?"

"Just wait." Lauren knelt down and unwrapped her bundle. A kitten, little more than a few weeks old, opened its eyes and meowed sleepily. Miss Molly whinnied in response.

As Wade's mouth gaped, the horse put its head down and nudged the kitten gently, drawing a hiss for her efforts. That didn't seem to daunt Miss Molly in the slightest. She swiped her tongue over the black-and-white fur ball. As if resigned to the attention, the kitten stood patiently for another couple of swipes, then danced away to wind itself around Lauren's ankles.

"Well, I'll be darned," Wade said.

"I take it there was a cat in the old barn," Lauren said.

"A big old tomcat," Wade confirmed. "He wasn't good for much but chasing mice."

"And apparently keeping Miss Molly company," Lauren suggested.

Wade recalled the number of times he'd found the old cat curled up on the windowsill in Miss Molly's stall. "You're right. I never paid a bit of attention to it, but when she was in the barn, he was always pretty much underfoot."

Ecstatic at the change already evident in Miss Molly, he grabbed Lauren by the waist and swung her around, then planted a solid kiss squarely on her mouth. "You're a certified genius," he declared.

"I wish I could take full credit, but Caitlyn's the one who brought the kitten for me to see," she told him. "Miss Molly reacted the instant she heard the first meow, and I knew we were on to something."

"Still, you were the one who said from the beginning that the horse was homesick. I thought you were nuts."

She patted his cheek. "I do like a man who can admit his mistakes."

"I've made my share," he agreed. "And I own up to them when I do."

"Will you own up to the fact that you misjudged Cole?" she asked, her tone still light.

Even so, the out-of-the-blue question spoiled Wade's mood. Davis embodied everything he hated about the rich. "Why would I want to admit to a thing like that? Were you hoping that if I was in a mellow mood, I'd forget all about what he did?"

"Not forget," she insisted. "I thought you might consider being fair."

"Fair?" he scoffed. "Was it fair of him to abandon a woman who was pregnant with his child? I imagine Cassie didn't consider that fair."

"Cole didn't know about the pregnancy," Lauren reminded him patiently. "His father and Cassie's mother saw to that. And Cassie was just a kid. She was scared, so she ran away."

"Cole sure as hell knew it was a possibility, unless you're saying he was too dumb to know where babies come from."

"Wade," she protested.

His frustration with the topic mounted. "Why are you pushing so hard for this, especially tonight, when we have other things we could be celebrating, like Miss Molly's recovery?"

"It's important to me that you get along with my friends."

"Okay," he said with a resigned sigh. "I can understand that and I can be polite when the circumstances call for it. But that's all I can promise where Cole Davis is concerned.''

She lifted a hand and rested it against his cheek, her expression a mixture of sympathy and regret. ''Cole is not the one who left you all those years ago,'' she said quietly.

''Dammit, I know that,'' he all but shouted. ''Never mind.'' He whirled around and walked away.

''Wade, where are you going?''

''I don't know,'' he said without breaking stride. ''Someplace that isn't here.'' Someplace where a woman he was beginning to love wouldn't be nagging him to relinquish the bitter hold his past had on him.

Lauren watched Wade walk away and sighed heavily. She had to get through to him—not just about Cole, but also about letting go of all the demons that haunted him. Otherwise, the two of them didn't stand a chance, not once he learned the truth about her.

Picking up the kitten, she stroked the soft fur absentmindedly. ''What am I going to do about him?'' she asked the kitten and Miss Molly. Neither of them offered any answers—at least none she could interpret.

As she walked away to return Good Golly to the office, Miss Molly snorted in protest. Lauren regarded her with amusement.

''I'll bring the kitten back in the morning,'' she promised. ''If I leave her with you overnight, I'm afraid you'll lick her to death. Now go eat some of your oats.''

For the first time in memory, the horse actually did as Lauren had requested, poking her head into the feed bag.

But her success with Miss Molly was small comfort

as Lauren sat on the porch back at Wade's waiting for him to return. When he still wasn't back by midnight, she went up to the main house to sleep in her own bed.

After a few restless, wasted hours of trying to sleep, she was in the kitchen before dawn and had the coffee brewing when Karen wandered in.

"How nice to see you at my kitchen table for a change," Karen said, regarding her with curiosity. "And even better, there's coffee. As soon as I get my first sip, I'll ask what you're doing here, so be prepared."

Lauren had been ready for the cross-examination from the moment she'd come downstairs. She knew she wasn't going to get away with any evasions, either.

Karen tipped up her cup, drank, and studied Lauren over the rim. "You look like hell," she noted eventually.

"Thanks so much."

"Didn't you get any sleep?"

Lauren shook her head.

"I guess you've gotten a little too used to sleeping in Wade's bed," Karen suggested. "So what brings you back up here? Did you two have a fight?"

Lauren thought back over the scene in the barn, then nodded. "I guess you could call it that. I was pushing him about something I thought was important. He got mad and walked out."

"Not exactly a give-and-take," Karen said.

"Not exactly."

"Want to tell me the issue?"

"I want to, but it's Wade's private business. He already thinks I discuss our relationship too much with my friends."

Karen's eyes widened. "Who else would you discuss it with, if not us?"

"I think his point is that I shouldn't be divulging any intimate details at all. It's a privacy thing with him. Ironically, I can understand where he's coming from."

"Because you've had most of your life the last ten years splashed on the front page of the tabloids," Karen concluded.

"Exactly."

"Does he know about that?"

"Not unless he's keeping it to himself. I don't think he has a clue what I used to do before I returned here."

"And now you're afraid that secret is going to come back to bite you in the butt," Karen guessed.

"Oh, yeah, big-time," Lauren said fervently.

"Maybe I gave you the wrong advice about that," Karen said guiltily.

"No, the advice was perfectly sound. It's just that there were things neither of us knew, things that might make it difficult for Wade to accept me once he knows the truth."

"Then tell him and face the music. Lay all your cards on the table before he finds out some other way. Frankly, I'm amazed someone hasn't let something slip before now."

"Me, too," Lauren admitted. "But is this the best time to spill everything, when he's already upset with me?"

"There might never be a good time. And Wade does care about you—the real you—doesn't he? You are sure of that now, aren't you?"

"Not that I have a lot of reason to trust my own judgment, but yes. Unless he's the biggest con artist of all time and has known who I was from the beginning, then Wade doesn't want anything from me except me. He doesn't even seem to think I have two nickels to rub together. The money, by the way, is another issue. He thinks he has very valid reasons for judging all the wealthy to be decadent and irresponsible. And when Jake very matter-of-factly spilled the beans about Cole and Cassie's situation, the story seemed to reinforce Wade's beliefs.''

"Oh my gosh, is that why the two of you went rushing out of there the other day? I thought you'd suddenly decided you needed to be alone."

Lauren blushed. "Well, that was one reason, but it was Jake's slip about his parents' belated marriage that really got us out of there."

"Did you explain the circumstances about why Cole didn't marry Cassie?"

"Not in great detail. He didn't want to hear it, anyway."

"Then I'll tell him," Karen said. "He can't go on blaming Cole for what happened, especially not if it's going to cause a rift between him and our friends. I will not have you coming back here only to get involved with someone who refuses to socialize with the rest of us."

Karen's gaze suddenly narrowed. "If the issue is money, why doesn't he resent Grady?"

"I'm not entirely sure," Lauren admitted. "But he thinks Grady's a decent guy and he's crazy about you. I think he's simply chosen to overlook the size of your bank account."

"Well, he'd better learn to overlook money altogether. It's not important—at least it shouldn't be. And it certainly shouldn't be the thing that stands between two people and their happiness."

"Amen to that," Lauren said. Now she just had to come up with some way to convince Wade of it.

Wade was tired and cranky and hungover when he got back to the Blackhawk ranch in the morning. He was almost relieved that Lauren wasn't at the house to see him in this sorry state.

Only after he'd showered, shaved and forced down some food and coffee did he begin to worry about where she might be. During the hour or so of sobriety he'd had before the beers at the Heartbreak had caught up with him, he'd managed to admit to himself that he was being totally unreasonable about Cole Davis. Nobody knew better than he did that a man shouldn't be judged on a first impression or on a past over which he'd had no control. Right before he'd gotten stinking drunk and taken a room in town for the night, he'd vowed to admit that to Lauren. He intended to keep that vow…assuming he could find her.

She wasn't in the barn, and when Wade checked the main house, Karen regarded him with an unmistakably cool expression and said she had no idea where Lauren had gone.

"Care for a cup of coffee?" she asked. "You look as if you could use it."

"Sure," he said, reluctantly taking a seat at the table and watching Karen warily.

Karen handed him the coffee, then took a seat opposite him. "You're the second person I've dealt with this morning who evidently had a lousy night."

"Oh?"

"Lauren looked like she hadn't gotten a wink of sleep."

Before he could comment on that or apologize for

his role in it, Karen seared him with a look. "I don't like seeing my friends upset."

"I'm sorry."

"I'm not the one who needs to hear that," she said.

He nodded. "Which is precisely why I came looking for her."

Her eyes softened then, and she gave him a more approving look. "Good. Then I don't need to break your kneecaps or anything."

"I notice you didn't say you'd have Grady do it," he said.

"Absolutely not. I fight my own battles…and my friends'," she added pointedly. "If I hadn't been satisfied with your answer, I would have taken pleasure in making you suffer."

He knew better than to grin. "I'll keep that in mind."

"See that you do. Now get out of here and resolve this before it gets out of hand."

He did allow himself a chuckle at that. "Yes, ma'am."

With his head still pounding, he walked slowly back toward the barn. Since Lauren's car was still parked beside his place, she had to be around here somewhere. A masculine curse from the paddock behind the barn had him racing around the side of the building. He skidded to a stop, his breath lodged in his throat as he took in the scene.

Grady was halfway over the fence, his face ashen as Lauren waved him off. She had a saddle on Midnight's back, but the huge horse wasn't one bit happy about it. He repeatedly reared up, his hooves slicing through the air with deadly potential for disaster.

"Lauren, get the hell out of there," Wade ordered, his voice low.

She didn't even spare him a glance. Instead, her entire focus was on Midnight, and even Wade had to admit that was where it belonged under the circumstances. With one hand on the horse's reins, she kept up a nonstop barrage of soft coaxing. The wild-eyed horse was having none of it.

Wade thought for a split second that his heart was going to pound so hard it would knock right through the wall of his chest. Never in his entire life had he been so terrified. If Lauren got out of there in one piece, he was going to be sorely tempted to kill her himself.

"She's absolutely fearless," Grady murmured, awe in his voice.

"She's a freaking lunatic," Wade retorted.

"I thought so, too, at first, but watch. Midnight's starting to listen to her. He's settling down."

Wade didn't see it. He could barely even make himself look at the scene. "Five seconds," he muttered. "Then I'm going to go in there and bodily drag her out."

"You'll do no such thing," Grady ordered. "Not if you expect to keep working for me."

"Then I'll quit," Wade said, hoisting himself onto the railing.

He was about to swing over and drop to the ground, when he felt Grady's hand on his arm.

"Look," his boss said quietly.

Midnight was perfectly still. He'd allowed Lauren close enough to drape an arm over his neck. When she held out a cube of sugar, he took it from her as calmly as if he hadn't been close to killing her not even seconds before.

Even so, Wade didn't breathe again until Lauren had removed the saddle, patted the horse on his rump and sent him off to the pasture.

"Nice work," Grady called out to her.

The praise was met with a tense smile. "It was a little dicey there for a minute," she said, her gaze cutting to Wade.

"Dicey?" he retorted as his heartbeat finally began to slow to something approaching normal. He saw her tense and softened his expression. "You scared the daylights out of me."

"To tell you the truth, I scared the daylights out of me, too," she admitted.

Suddenly her knees wobbled. Wade hit the ground and caught her just before she collapsed in a heap. She gave him an uneasy look.

"I guess the adrenaline's worn off," she murmured.

"Guess so," he agreed, fighting the desire to kiss her senseless.

A spark flared in her eyes, and without warning she shoved against his chest with all her might. "Put me down," she demanded. "I'm furious with you."

Grady grinned. "I don't think I'm needed for this part. I think I'll be going now."

"Smart man," Wade said as he struggled to keep Lauren in place. He gazed into her flashing eyes. "Okay, darlin', let's compare notes. You're furious with me—rightfully so, I might add—and I am sorely aggravated with you—also entirely justified. Let's call it even, okay?"

"Not on your life, you pigheaded coward."

"Coward?" Wade repeated softly. If a man had

made that accusation, he'd be lying in the dust with a swollen jaw by now.

"When we have a disagreement, you don't get to run off. Mature adults who care about each other talk things out."

"You're right," he agreed, clearly taking the wind out of her sails.

"You recognize that?" she asked skeptically.

"Now I do," he said, regarding her solemnly.

"Good."

"Since we're agreed on that," he said. "Let's calmly discuss what just happened here."

She slid her fingers into his hair and lowered her mouth until it was almost against his. "Let's not," she murmured.

The kiss pretty much settled things for the time being, but Wade didn't doubt for a second that it was not a precursor to smooth sailing from here on out. That image of Lauren within a hairsbreadth of getting herself trampled was going to stay with him for a long time to come. He didn't intend to give the horse a second chance to complete the job.

Chapter Eleven

"I want to sell Midnight," Wade announced as he and Grady sat at the kitchen table late that night. Lauren and Karen were having their weekly dinner with the Calamity Janes, this time at Tony's. Gina was cooking some new pasta recipe she'd dreamed up so she could try it out on her friends before springing it on the customers.

"Because of what happened earlier," Grady said, his expression every bit as grim as Wade's tone.

"Of course because of that. Midnight could have trampled Lauren to death, and she's too stubborn to admit that her life was in any danger. If it's up to her, she'll be right back in there tomorrow."

"Because it's what she does," Grady reminded him. "She's good at it. She won't appreciate you taking this chance away from her. Her work with Midnight could go a long way toward giving her a reputation for being able to work with troubled animals.''

''At least she'll be alive.'' Wade retorted.

''If I agree to this—and I'm not saying I do—will you tell her before you sell him? You owe her that,'' Grady said.

Wade sighed. ''I suppose,'' he conceded, dreading the conversation. He knew, just as Grady obviously did, that Lauren wasn't going to thank him for trying to protect her. ''I'll have to find some way to make her understand.''

Grady gave him a commiserating look. ''I don't envy you that conversation. Midnight is a great horse, one of the best I've ever seen. He has a lot of heart. It'll be a shame to lose him, but if it's what you have to do for your own peace of mind, then put Midnight in the next horse auction over in Cheyenne.'' He grinned. ''And let me know how your conversation with Lauren turns out. I'd like to be a fly on the wall for that one.''

Wade wasn't nearly as relieved by Grady's acquiescence as he had expected to be. After all, the man was letting him get rid of a magnificent, promising stallion on what amounted to a whim. If Lauren's safety hadn't been involved, Wade would never have considered selling the horse. And if he'd been the one in the paddock taking the risks himself, he would have considered it part of the job.

Clearly some of his lack of enthusiasm could be attributed to losing a potentially great stud. The rest, no doubt, could be blamed on the certain knowledge that Lauren was likely to take a verbal strip out of his hide when she found out. He wasn't looking forward to that nearly as eagerly as Grady seemed to be.

"Thanks," he said sincerely. "I owe you, Grady."

"You do, indeed," the other man said.

"If you don't mind, I think I'll wait for Lauren on the porch. I might as well get this conversation over with tonight."

"Good idea. Besides, I'm pretty sure there's nothing out there she can throw at you the way there would be in here."

Wade winced. "You think it's going to be that bad?"

"Oh, yeah," Grady confirmed. "In fact, I'm betting it'll be worse."

Wade regarded him wryly. "Thanks for the encouragement."

"Anytime, pal. If you need somebody to patch you up later, give a holler. I'll make sure the first-aid kit is fully stocked."

"Very funny," Wade muttered as he went on out to the porch to wait.

When Karen and Lauren drove up a half hour later, he could hear the two of them giggling as they emerged from the car. It made him wonder what went on at these gabfests of theirs. He sighed. That hardly mattered now.

The pair of them stopped in their tracks when they hit the bottom step and spotted him.

"Hey, Wade, how are you doing?" Karen asked politely.

Lauren said nothing, but her gaze never left him. It was as if she sensed right off that she wasn't going to like his reason for being there.

"I'm fine," he told Karen. "Did you all have a good night?"

"We always do," Lauren retorted with a hint of defiance. It was not a good sign.

"How was Gina's pasta?" he asked, hoping that neutral turf would ease the tension.

Lauren wasn't buying it for a second. "Gina's food was fabulous, as always, but somehow I don't think that's what's on your mind."

"No," he agreed.

"Well, I assume you're not waiting out here for me," Karen said cheerfully. "I'll leave you two and go see what my man is up to. Come on in when you're through, though. I have some news I'd like to share."

"Fine," Lauren said distractedly, her gaze still locked on Wade.

When they were alone, Wade said to Lauren, "Well, are you just going to stand there all night?"

"That depends," she said.

"On?"

"What you're doing here."

"We need to talk," he said.

"I got that much. About?"

"Midnight."

"There's nothing to discuss. I'm just doing my job."

"Not anymore," he said curtly, annoyed that she had voiced what his own sentiments would have been had the shoe been on the other foot.

Her furious gaze cut straight through him. "I beg your pardon. Are you firing me?"

"Nope," he said quietly. "I'm selling Midnight."

"Over my dead body," she snapped right back.

"It's a done deal. Grady has agreed."

"Do you have a buyer?"

"Not yet."

"Then I'll buy him. Name your price."

"You can't afford it," he retorted.

Her mouth opened, but she snapped it closed again as the apparent reality set in. She was visibly trembling with outrage as she stalked up the steps and faced him.

"Then I'll have Grady buy out your share," she said. "If I can't talk him into it, I'm sure Karen can."

Wade honestly hadn't anticipated that response. He hadn't discussed it with Grady, either, but his gut told him she was right. She could pull it off. Grady would go along with whatever Karen wanted. Family would rate over a mere employee or even business partner. It was hard to argue with that kind of loyalty.

"Don't do this," he begged. "That horse almost killed you today."

"But he didn't, and it wasn't his fault. He's getting better every day. Your instincts were exactly right when you and Grady bought him. He's magnificent."

"He's dangerous," Wade said flatly.

"Only because he was so badly mistreated in the past. He's scared, Wade, the same way you are right now. You're acting without thinking."

"I've thought of nothing else all day long," he countered. "You have no idea what went through my mind when I saw you within a fraction of an inch of being trampled." Even now the memory was enough to send a shudder through him.

Lauren finally walked over to stand in front of him. "I won't beg you not to do this, Wade," she said quietly. "But if you do, I will never forgive you. Moreover, I don't think you'll ever be able to forgive yourself."

"I will," he said defiantly, even though her solemn expression shook him to his core. "All I'll have to do is remember what I saw."

"Then it doesn't matter to you how I feel?"

"Of course, but—"

She cut him off. "Don't do this, Wade. It's wrong."

"Dammit, Lauren," he muttered, thoroughly frustrated by her refusal to listen to reason.

"You know it is," she persisted. When he didn't immediately argue, she came closer, though she was still careful not to touch him. "Tell me this, if you had been the one working with him today, would you want to sell him?"

There it was, he thought with a sigh. The cool logic he had feared. She had pegged it and put him squarely between a rock and a hard place. If he said yes, she would never believe him. If he said no, she would blame it on his lack of faith in her skill. Desolation washed through him.

"I couldn't bear it if anything happened to you," he said finally, his voice raw.

"Nor I, if it happened to you, but we can't take our fears out on Midnight. He's so close, Wade. Please give him this chance. Give *me* this chance."

The urgency in her voice got to him. "Why is this so important to you?"

"I need to prove to myself that this is something I can do," she said. "I need to know I can make a career out of it. If I give up on Midnight, who would ever trust me to work with a horse again?"

It was the same argument Grady had tried to use to persuade him. Rationally, he understood their reasoning, but that couldn't cut through the fear.

"I would trust you," he said readily. "You know how good you are, Lauren. We both do."

"Then let me finish this job."

Wade struggled with himself, with his fears, but it

was the expression in her eyes that won him over. She was ready to fight for this chance, perhaps even ready to walk away from him if he didn't give it to her. In the end, he couldn't take the chance that she would make good on that threat.

"You'll work with him only if I'm around," he said slowly.

A smile tugged at the corners of her mouth. "Yes."

"And if I say it's over for the day, you won't argue with me," he added.

"Whatever you say," she agreed eagerly.

Wade wondered wryly how long that would last, but for now it was a concession. "Okay, then. I'll tell Grady we're keeping Midnight."

She launched herself into his arms, then smothered his face with kisses. For a moment, Wade allowed himself to bask in the pure pleasure of the sensation, but then worry crowded out pleasure. He was going to be on his knees every single night from here on out praying that he hadn't just made the worst mistake of his life.

Lauren was triumphant, but she was careful not to gloat when she reminded Wade of their promise to Karen.

"She said she had news."

"We could wait and hear it in the morning," he suggested, clearly eager to get up to his place where they could finish making up in bed.

Lauren was tempted, but determined not to give in. "Oh no you don't. We have news of our own to share. You need to let Grady know what you've decided about Midnight." She wasn't taking any chance that he'd try to wiggle out of it by morning.

He scooted her off his lap and stood up. "Let's get this over with then."

When they walked into the kitchen, Karen beamed at them. Grady stared at them with a dazed expression.

"Okay," Lauren prodded. "What's the news? Obviously it's put Grady into shock."

"We're having a baby," Karen announced without preamble.

"Oh my gosh, that's wonderful," Lauren said, rushing across the room to gather her friend into an embrace.

"Congratulations," Wade said, shaking Grady's hand.

Grady still looked as if he'd been poleaxed. Lauren chuckled and planted a kiss on his cheek. "It can't be that much of a shock. Surely, you do know how babies get made. And it's not like the two of you aren't always sneaking off to be together."

Grady stared at her, then looked back at his wife. "A baby? You're sure?"

Karen nodded, regarding him with amusement. "The doctor confirmed it when I was in town today. And if you don't get over here and kiss me, I'm going to get on the phone and call your grandfather. I know he's been waiting to hear this news."

"Waiting? He's been pestering me ever since our wedding day," Grady said. He scooped his wife out of her chair and twirled her around, then set her back on her feet, his expression suddenly worried. "That was probably a bad idea. Maybe you should sit back down. Do you need anything? Can I get you something to drink? Something to eat? Maybe you should rest."

Karen regarded Lauren with a frantic expression. "If

this is what it's going to be like around here for the next seven months, I'm moving out.''

"He'll settle down," Lauren soothed, then shot a warning look at Grady. "Won't you?"

Karen shook her head. "Why do men insist on being so blasted overprotective? We're not fragile little creatures."

"Tell me about it," Lauren said with a pointed look toward Wade.

"Hey, it's not the same thing at all," Wade protested. "Having a baby is perfectly natural. It's not as scary as seeing a woman you love dancing around under the flying hooves of a horse."

His comment brought all conversation to a complete halt. Lauren's mouth gaped. When she could finally gather her wits, she said, "Did you just say you loved me?"

"He did," Karen confirmed eagerly. "I heard him."

"Sounded that way to me, too," Grady added, clearly amused by the turn of events.

"I didn't…" Wade's protest trailed off. "Okay, fine. I admit it. I love you."

Lauren grinned at him. "What a gracious way to put it. My heart's all aflutter."

He scowled at her. "I can still take it back."

"You can try," she teased. "But I won't believe you. The die is cast."

"Of course, we haven't heard where you stand on the subject," Grady pointed out.

Wade regarded her with evident fascination. "Yes, by all means, let's hear how you feel about it."

"Are we talking love in general?" she inquired, watching Wade's increasing frustration with amusement.

"Whatever," he said.

"Or how I feel about you specifically?" she added.

"Maybe you'd like to be alone again for this," Grady suggested. "Karen and I have something we could be celebrating upstairs anyway."

"All that *celebrating* is how she got pregnant," Lauren reminded them. "Besides, I want to share a toast with the expectant couple, once Wade and I resolve this little matter of who loves whom."

She was about to tell Wade exactly how she felt about him, when the phone rang. All four of them stared at it in dismay, but eventually Karen grabbed it.

"Yes, she's right here," she told the caller, then made a face as she handed the phone to Lauren. "Jason."

Wade went perfectly still as Lauren accepted it. Because she couldn't bring herself to face him as she talked to her agent, she stepped outside.

"Jason, how many different ways can I say no?" she asked, not even trying to hide her annoyance.

"I just hate to see you making a huge mistake like this," he said. "I don't want you to wake up in a few months or a year with regrets."

She glanced through the screen door and saw Wade sitting there stiffly, his face looking as if it had been carved from granite. Karen and Grady were making a halfhearted attempt to engage him in conversation, but his gaze was riveted on Lauren.

"No regrets," she assured Jason. "Not one. If anything changes in the future, I'll get in touch with you. In the meantime, scratch me off your client list."

"If I do that, I can't promise I'll be able to do a thing for you," he said. "It's a fast-paced business, Lauren. People forget."

"Not if I'm half as good as you're always telling me I am," she retorted.

"Then your decision is final?"

"Isn't that what I've been telling you for weeks now?"

Jason sighed. "Okay, then, I'll take you at your word. If you change your mind, call me."

"I won't change my mind," she said with conviction. Whatever happened with Wade, she was more certain than ever that her home was right here in Wyoming. Hollywood seemed a million miles away and a lifetime ago.

Slowly she hung up and went back inside, a smile plastered on her face. Wade didn't return it as she sat back down beside him.

"Lauren, you were just about to tell us— Ouch," Grady said, scowling at his wife. "Well, she was."

"I think the moment's lost for right now," Karen said. "But I definitely want that toast you promised, Lauren."

Lauren dutifully lifted her glass of tea and tried to recapture at least a little of the celebratory mood from earlier. "To the new little Blackhawk. He or she is coming into a terrific home. Congratulations, you two."

"Congratulations," Wade echoed, though his tone was flat. He sipped his tea, then stood up. Without so much as looking at Lauren, he said, "I've got to be getting back down to my place."

"I'll go with you," Lauren said.

He seemed about to protest, but the words died on his lips. Relieved by that, she followed him to the door.

"Good night, you two. I really am happy for you,"

she said to Grady and Karen, who were watching her and Wade uneasily.

"Thanks," Karen said, then added pointedly, "See you in the morning."

There was no mistaking that it was anything other than a command.

"First thing," Lauren agreed.

Wade was silent as they walked toward his place. More important, he was also very careful to avoid so much as brushing up against her. She could feel the anger or tension or whatever it was practically radiating off him.

"Okay, just go ahead and say it," she said finally.

"Say what?"

"Whatever's on your mind."

He whirled on her. "Okay, fine. I want to know why that man is still calling you."

"I can't control what Jason does," she replied reasonably. "I'm not calling him. And you've heard me tell him that I'm not interested in anything he has to tell me."

"You insist there's nothing between you, but how am I supposed to buy that when he hasn't given up?"

"Because I'm telling you the truth," she said flatly. "Are you saying you don't trust me?"

He frowned at the challenge. "No," he said eventually. "But if he continues to harass you, I think you should tell the sheriff. There are laws about that kind of thing."

She almost chuckled, but then she realized he was dead serious. "Wade, I can't do that."

"Why not? Unless he means more to you than you're admitting."

"I don't know how else to say this, not when you're

being as pigheaded as he is. Jason doesn't mean anything to me, not personally anyway. He's a former business associate for whom I still have a great deal of respect. That's it.''

"What kind of business associate keeps on calling after he's been told to give up?''

"The kind who's persistent," she said, aware that Wade couldn't understand any man pestering a woman unless it was because he wanted her. He had no frame of reference for a man in a business where persistence was not only a virtue but a necessity.

He scowled down at her. "You claim he's not after you. Then what the hell does he want?''

Lauren weighed her reply carefully. This was a chance to tell Wade everything, but if she did it now when he was already irritated, he was likely to blow it all out of proportion. No, she decided, it would be better to wait until he was in the right frame of mind—whatever that was. At least, she could tell him a part of the truth.

"Jason wants me to come back to work. That's it.''

Wade seemed to chew over that explanation for a bit, then finally nodded. "And you're sure that's all it is? He's not harassing you or stalking you or something?''

"Absolutely not.''

"And you can handle it?''

She grinned at him. "I can handle the likes of Jason any day of the week. You're the one who's giving me fits.''

His lips twitched then. "Oh, I am, am I?'' He seemed very pleased with himself. "In what way?''

"You've kept me out here wasting time talking about a man who means absolutely nothing to me, when I could be inside making love with a man who does matter.''

He slid his hand into her hair and tilted her head up. ''And that annoys you?''

''Frustrates me,'' she corrected.

''Would a kiss help?''

''It would definitely be a start in the right direction,'' she confirmed.

With tantalizing restraint, he slowly lowered his head until his lips were just above hers. She could already feel the promised heat, but he refused the contact she was craving.

''Has anybody ever told you that you're a tease?'' she murmured.

''Not nearly often enough,'' he whispered just as his mouth settled on hers.

There was something greedy and raw and needy about the kiss. The sensations exploded through her. Suddenly Lauren felt as if she were falling…falling from the topmost peak of a mountain…falling in love.

She rocked back on her heels and captured Wade's face in her hands. She gazed deep into his eyes.

''We have some unfinished business,'' she told him.

''You bet we do,'' he said.

''Not that,'' she said with a quick smile. ''From earlier. I love you, Wade Owens.'' She saw his eyes go dark, saw the quick flash of heat. ''Just so you know.''

''It's a darn good thing,'' he murmured. ''I'd hate to be in water this deep all by myself.''

She searched his face. ''Then you meant what you said up at the house? You do love me?''

He grinned at her. ''It scares the hell out of me, but yes, darlin', I do.''

Lauren's heart soared. And as long as she didn't let herself think about the secret that could destroy them, it would keep right on soaring.

Chapter Twelve

"So, did you and Lauren patch things up last night?" Grady inquired when Wade rode out with him the next morning to check fence lines.

Wade thought of the raw passion that had kept them both awake for half the night. "You could say that."

"After you agreed not to sell Midnight, I assume."

Wade realized that they'd never gotten to that topic the night before, but he could read the gloating expression on Grady's face. "Yeah, she convinced me it was a bad idea."

Grady chuckled. "I'll just bet she did."

"Hey, I won a couple of concessions from her," Wade protested. "She'll only work with him when I'm around, and if something looks too risky, she'll stop when I say so."

"She actually agreed to that?"

"You bet," Wade said, then shrugged. "I imagine

it won't take her more than a couple of days to forget all about it, though.''

"Yep, you know Lauren, all right." Grady turned a penetrating look on Wade. "Were you serious about being in love with her? Karen's going to take you apart bit by bit if you were just playing games.''

"No games," Wade assured him. "No woman has ever twisted me into knots the way Lauren does.''

"You thinking marriage?''

Wade froze, drawing his horse to a dead stop. "Marriage?" He echoed the word as if he'd never heard it before. It hadn't come up the night before. He was certain of that. If it had, he would have blasted the idea right out of the water. He was equally sure of that.

"That's usually the next step," Grady said. His gaze narrowed. "Unless you were playing games, after all.''

"It's just that I never thought that far ahead," Wade said defensively. "What the heck do I have to offer a woman?''

"You have a good job, a place to live," Grady reminded him. "You have plans for the future. And the way I hear it, you have the most important thing of all—you love her.''

"Is that enough?" Wade said. He thought about his plans for the future. Only with Grady's encouragement had he actually begun to dream of owning his own horse-breeding operation a few years down the road. He still couldn't quite believe that it was within his reach. Until he'd come to the Blackhawk ranch, he'd always assumed he would spend his life drifting from one job to another.

"I suppose the only one who can answer whether it's enough is Lauren," Grady said. "A few months ago, I might not have thought so, but I've seen a lot of changes in her. Being here—being with you—has grounded her. Something tells me she'll think it's plenty.''

Marriage to Lauren. An image of her all dressed up in yards and yards of white satin with a gossamer-sheer veil trailing down her back from a tiara of pearls made his heart hammer inside his chest. To know that she was his forever? He wanted that. Wanted it more than anything he'd ever longed for.

Was it really within his reach? he wondered. A few weeks ago he'd never even imagined telling a woman he loved her and hearing the same words spoken back to him. Yet last night he'd told Lauren just that. She'd admitted she loved him, too. And she'd shown him just how much all night long.

But marriage was permanent. It was forever, and he rarely thought too far beyond tomorrow. Besides, he'd never even seen a good example of it. His own mother had never married, preferring the kind of casual relationships that wouldn't put her heart at risk again after what had happened with Wade's father. His daddy had been married for years, just not to Wade's mother, and it hadn't stopped him from chasing anything in skirts. With those two as his role models, was it any wonder he was skeptical that he could make it work?

One thing he knew for sure, he'd better be a lot more certain than he was right now before he risked making that kind of commitment. If he ever did get married, he wanted the kind of marriage Karen and Grady had. Even a drifting wrangler with a background like his could see that what they had would endure.

"Do you have any idea how lucky you are?" he asked Grady. "You and Karen, clearly you were destined to be together."

Grady regarded him with surprise. "That's how it seems to you?"

"Sure," Wade said, startled by Grady's response. "Am I wrong?"

"I hope not," Grady said. "But it wasn't always that way and not a day goes by that I don't thank the Lord for what we've found." At Wade's puzzled look, Grady added, "You know Karen was a widow when we met?"

"No," Wade admitted, stunned by the news. He'd assumed they were childhood sweethearts, because they seemed so attuned to each other.

"Well, she was. And I had been her husband's worst enemy," Grady revealed. "There were a whole lot of issues we had to work through before she could begin to trust me. I'm here to tell you that anything that comes up between you and Lauren would be a piece of cake by comparison." He grinned. "But you're right about one thing—it was worth every bit of the struggle, and I don't intend to let Karen regret the decision she made. Not ever."

When the time came, Wade wanted to be able to make the same kind of vow where Lauren was concerned. It would kill him if he ever gave her any cause to regret getting mixed up with him.

Despite Grady's protests, Karen had insisted on doing her chores around the ranch.

"I told him if he tried to turn me into an invalid for the next seven months, I'd have to strangle him," she had explained to Lauren as they'd shared a cup of coffee earlier.

"Well, you'd better get out there and slave away," Lauren had told her, eager to get her out of the house so she could start making calls to the other Calamity Janes. She needed time alone if she was going to pull off a surprise lunch to celebrate the news about the baby.

"But I have questions for you," Karen protested, refusing to budge from the table. "I want to know what happened between you and Wade after you left here."

"Quite a lot, as a matter of fact, but you can wait to hear all the details," she said. When Karen still showed no evidence of leaving, Lauren added bluntly, "Will you please just go away?"

"Ah," Karen said, clearly amused by the less-than diplomatic dismissal. "Then you *are* trying to get rid of me?"

"Yes," Lauren said emphatically.

Karen had laughed. "Okay, then. I'm out of here." When she reached the door, she turned back for one last parting shot. "Just make sure somebody brings chocolate. I have a craving."

So much for any surprise, Lauren thought. "I guarantee there will be lots and lots of chocolate."

She made all the calls within a half hour, giving away as little as possible as she cajoled Gina into making lasagna and Cassie into picking up a chocolate cake with double-fudge frosting from Stella's.

"Be here in one hour," she ordered Emma when she caught up with her at the office. "Not a minute longer."

"I'm supposed to meet with a client in an hour."

Only Emma would risk protesting Lauren's command.

"Is he dying?" Lauren asked.

"No."

"About to be charged with murder?"

"No, but—"

"Then he can wait. Be here. And pick up some balloons on the way. And some chocolate ice cream, a gallon of it. The good kind with lots of fat and calories." She hung up before Emma could argue with her.

Satisfied that she was going to pull off the impromptu celebration, Lauren set the dining-room table with the fancy china and silver, then went onto the porch to wait for the party to come to her.

It didn't surprise her in the slightest that despite her protests Emma was the first to arrive. She exited the car with a handful of bobbing, multicolored balloons, a grocery bag filled with gourmet ice cream and a determined expression.

"What is this all about?" she demanded as Lauren led the way inside and put the ice cream into the freezer.

"You'll see."

"Tell me now or die," Emma ordered.

Lauren regarded her with an exaggerated frown. "Is that any way for an attorney to talk?"

"It is when one of her best friends is keeping secrets," Emma declared.

"Oh, hush, and help me spread these balloons around so it will look festive."

"Who's coming?" Emma asked.

"I've rounded up the usual suspects."

"You got Cassie and Gina to take off in the middle of the day? I'm impressed. How did you accomplish it? Blackmail?"

"Like I'd tell you if that's what I'd done. Besides, have you ever known one of us to be able to resist a party?" Lauren asked.

"Now that you mention it, no. Is the party for Karen?"

"Maybe."

"What are we celebrating?" Suddenly her eyes widened. "A baby? That's it, isn't it? Karen's going to have a baby?"

"My lips are sealed," Lauren insisted.

Emma's gaze turned diabolical. "Will they still be sealed if I start to tickle you?" she asked, advancing on Lauren. "It used to work like a charm at our slumber parties back in high school."

"I am no longer ticklish," Lauren insisted, hoping to discourage her, but backing away in case it didn't work.

"Then you won't mind if I try," Emma said.

Lauren yelped as Emma reached for her. She darted out of the dining room and was racing through the house when Gina came in and skidded to a stop just in time to prevent having her lasagna upended on the living-room rug.

"Help me," Lauren pleaded, laughing as she hid behind Gina. "There's a maniac after me."

Gina chuckled. "Why is Emma after you?"

"Because she won't tell me what we're all doing here," Emma said.

Gina's grin spread. "That is a good incentive. I think I'll put this dish right over here and join the chase."

"Hey," Karen shouted over the commotion. "Stop it right this second before you knock over all my furniture. I'll tell."

"Not till Cassie gets here," Lauren said sternly. "It's not fair to leave her out."

"Leave me out of what?" Cassie asked, coming in with a huge cake box.

"Can I tell?" Lauren pleaded, then stopped herself. "No, of course not. It's your news. You should tell."

"As if there's likely to be any surprise left to it after all this," Karen grumbled good-naturedly. "Okay, drumroll, please." She paused dramatically, then announced, "I'm going to have a baby."

Whoops of delight greeted the announcement, but even before the others could surround her, she gave Lauren a wicked look and added, "And Lauren's in love."

After that, there were so many questions, so many hugs, that Lauren's head was spinning. She grabbed Karen and pulled her from the fray. "This can't be good for the baby. Sit. I'll get lunch on the table." She leaned in closer to whisper, "And I'll get even with you for this."

Karen laughed. "Yes, I was sure you would."

Wade spent the entire day mulling over his conversation with Grady. That night, when he and Lauren met at his place for a quiet dinner alone, it was still on his mind.

Maybe because she was evidently in such a mellow mood—slightly tipsy, in fact—he concluded it was a perfect time to broach the subject of the future, at least in abstract terms.

When the dishes were done and they'd retreated to the porch, he studied her. In the fading sunlight, her skin was radiant. Unlike a lot of redheads, her fair skin hadn't freckled with all the exposure to the sun. It was still pale as cream, no doubt thanks to the sunscreen he saw her applying every ten seconds when she was outdoors. She'd drawn her hair up into a haphazard ponytail, from which curls escaped to tease her neck and her cheeks. She was without a doubt the most beautiful woman he'd ever seen.

And her mouth, ah, that mouth was pure temptation. He grew hard just thinking about its clever, wicked ways. As he studied her, her lips curved slowly and he realized she was staring at him with amusement.

"What?"

"That's what I should be asking you," she said. "You were studying me as if I were some sort of exotic specimen you had to report on."

"You are, you know. You're the most exotic creature I've ever met. You're sexy and mysterious and sometimes I have to wonder if I even know you at all."

Something that struck him as alarm flared briefly in her eyes, but was gone in a heartbeat. He couldn't be sure he'd even seen it at all.

"Of course you know me," she said, then gave him a dazzling smile. "Pretty much every inch of me, in fact."

"I'm talking about more than sex," he said.

"Okay," she said, her expression cautious. "What did you want to know?"

Everything, he thought with a neediness that surprised him. He wanted to know everything about her childhood, about her years in California, what kind of foods she liked, what her favorite color was. It sounded silly when he put it that way, but it was true. He wanted to know Lauren inside out, the way she seemed to know and understand him. She had gotten him to reveal secrets he'd never shared with another living soul, and she seemed able to see exactly how his past had affected the man he'd become, but he knew none of the same sort of secrets from her past. Had she deliberately kept them hidden, or had he simply never asked?

"Let's start with something simple," he said slowly, his gaze locked on her expressive face. "Do you realize that never once in all these weeks have you told me your last name?"

This time there was no mistaking the panic that flashed in her eyes, even though, once again, she covered it almost instantly. He watched and waited, growing increasingly flustered when she continued to hesitate. What was the big deal about a last name? Most people who dated shared that much from their first meeting.

Finally, the casual note in her voice sounding forced, she said, "It's Winters, Lauren Winters."

"You said that as if there was some sort of secret about it," he said, completely baffled by her uneasy reaction.

"No, of course not," she said hurriedly. "I guess I hadn't realized I'd never told you or that you hadn't heard it from Grady or Karen. Funny how you can completely forget about something like that if it's not out there at the very beginning, isn't it? How embarrassing to think we've slept together and you didn't even know who I was."

She was babbling. Wade had never seen her react so nervously...and to what? He'd just asked her last name. Considering the fact that they'd shared a bed, this hardly seemed important. He was missing something here, something important, but maybe it could wait for a moment when she was less edgy. Her mellow mood of a few minutes ago had certainly vanished.

"Come on over here, Lauren Winters," he coaxed. "Let's get reacquainted."

The full-fledged smile she bestowed on him was worth sacrificing a few more probing questions. She slipped into his lap and settled her head on his shoulder with a contented sigh.

"This is lovely," she murmured.

It was, Wade thought. More than lovely, in fact. It was just about perfect. If only he didn't have this increasingly sick sensation in the pit of his stomach that it was all going to blow up in his face.

Lauren had thought for a few minutes that her heart was going to leap straight out of her chest. When Wade had pressed her to reveal her last name, she had been consumed by a terrible sense of dread. It had taken every ounce of courage she possessed to say it aloud, to force a nonchalant tone into her voice.

Only when it had become clear that the name meant nothing to him had she been able to breathe again. Only then had her heartbeat returned to normal. Obviously Wade didn't follow movies or the gossip about celebrities that had been a mainstay of her life for so many years. She had forgotten that there were people in the world to whom all of that meant less than nothing.

Why, then, hadn't she told him the rest? Maybe he wouldn't have realized just what being an actress meant. If he was so oblivious to that world, he might have accepted her past as easily as if she'd told him she'd been an accountant, as something of no consequence whatsoever.

But in her panic, she had frozen, and then the moment had passed. Now, cradled in his arms, she could almost convince herself that none of it mattered, that it would all turn out okay eventually.

"So," he began, his fingers grazing her cheek as he

gently brushed a wisp of hair away from her face, "where do you see this going?"

Her heart leaped. She wanted to be absolutely clear on what he was asking. "This?"

"You and me."

She considered her answer. "Truthfully, I've been so content with where we are, I haven't thought about where we might be headed. Have you?"

"Not until today," he admitted.

"What happened today?"

"Grady asked if I intended to marry you." He grinned at her. "He was being very big brotherly about it."

"What did you tell him?" she asked, her heart in her throat.

"The same as what you said, that I hadn't been thinking that far ahead." His gaze captured hers. "Should we, though? Should we think about it?"

He looked so worried, so sweetly concerned about doing the right thing. "Only if you want to. I'm in no rush," she reassured him.

He scanned her face intently, then smiled. "Liar. I suspect you're the kind of woman who was born being in a rush."

"No, I wasn't," she said, then reconsidered.

After all, she hadn't been able to wait to finish school and take off. She had raced through high school with the same amount of impatience as Emma and Gina, eager to get out into the world. Of course, from the beginning they had been intent on making a name for themselves in their respective fields. She had only wanted to be away from Winding River. She had craved an adventure, but never in a million years had she imagined the kind of glamour and excitement that were in store for her. Nor had she known that eventually it would become such an albatross.

"Okay, maybe I was once," she told him. "But no more. Since I've come back, I've learned to take one day at a time, to linger over life's pleasures and savor them."

She glanced up just as a vivid orange sun slid below the horizon, leaving a sky streaked with brilliant color. "There," she said. "Just look at that. Have you ever seen anything more beautiful?"

"Yes," Wade murmured, his gaze never leaving her face. "You."

She reached up and touched his cheek. "You say the most amazing things. How did I ever get so lucky?"

He seemed surprised by her words. "You think you're the lucky one?"

"I *know* I am," she said. "I came back here hoping—no, *praying*—that I would find something that had been missing from my life, and here you are. Just like that."

He grinned. "Just like that, huh?"

"Okay, maybe not just like that," she said with a laugh. "We did have to get past all the animosity and distrust and your ego."

"*My* ego?" he echoed incredulously, obviously recalling her high-and-mighty attitude on the day they'd met.

"Well, you were way too sure of yourself that day you found me with Midnight," she reminded him.

"And you weren't?"

She laughed. "Me? I was docile as a lamb."

"My, but you do have a selective memory," he said. "But that's okay, as long as you remember one thing."

"What's that?"

"That you belong to me."

Lauren's gaze narrowed. "Belong?" she echoed.

"Okay," he said, a glimmer of amusement in his eyes. "Bad choice of words. I did not mean that in a possessive way. No, indeed. A commitment way, that's how I meant it."

"You want me to make a commitment to you?"

He hesitated, then nodded. "Yes, I guess I do."

"Now there's a firm response if ever I heard one," she teased. "Do you or don't you?"

"I do, darlin'," he said emphatically. "I most definitely do."

"And you're making this same kind of commitment to me?"

"Absolutely."

"Is this the kind of commitment where we agree not to see anyone else for the foreseeable future or is it the forever, happily-ever-after kind?"

She saw the muscle work in Wade's jaw as he wrestled with the question.

"Let's start with the foreseeable future and see where it takes us. Does that work for you?"

Well enough, she thought to herself. She could envision a foreseeable future that lasted through eternity. And she was pretty sure that without much effort, she could get Wade to see that, too...if only her past didn't surface and ruin it all.

Chapter Thirteen

Lauren took the morning off to drive into Winding River. After her conversation with Wade the night before, she wanted to talk to Emma. While all of her friends were sensible, Emma was the one who was the least romantic, the least likely to get caught up in the thrill of a relationship and forget the practicalities. Lauren had called her at dawn, aware that years of workaholic habits hadn't deserted Emma even after months back in Winding River. They had agreed to meet for breakfast at Stella's.

Lauren was in their favorite secluded booth in the back when Emma strolled in. Stella already had her coffee cup filled and had left her usual breakfast of cereal and a banana. Emma frowned at them.

"Am I that predictable?" she asked Lauren.

"We all are," Lauren lamented, picking at her usual bowl of strawberries with not even a dollop of milk in the bowl, much less cream. "And after all these years, if we tried to change, it would probably shock Stella so badly she'd have to retire."

Emma sighed and picked up her spoon. "Oh, well, at least it's healthy." She gazed at Lauren and waited. "Come on. You didn't call me at 6:00 a.m. just for my scintillating company. You were fine when I saw you yesterday, so something's obviously happened. Spit it out."

"That's what I love about you. You're so sympathetic."

"You didn't call me for sympathy, you called for my levelheaded advice—am I right?"

"Yes," Lauren agreed meekly.

"I can't give it if you don't tell me the problem."

"Okay, okay. I think I may have made a terrible mistake with Wade and I don't know how to fix it," she blurted.

Emma went absolutely still. "What kind of mistake? He's not hurting you, is he?"

Lauren felt the color drain from her face. She should have realized that would be Emma's greatest fear. Emma had dealt with too many domestic-violence tragedies in her law career, first in Denver, then with the shooting death that had kept her coming back to Winding River for months before she'd finally decided to stay.

"Absolutely not," she assured her friend. "I'm sorry. I should have been more careful. No, actually this is something *I* did. Or didn't do."

Emma's concerned expression eased. "You're not making a lot of sense," she said.

"I've kept things from him. I told you before that I never told him about my career in Hollywood. Apparently he's not a movie fan, so he still doesn't have a clue what I did when I lived in California.''

"And you think he's going to be furious when he finds out about the deception?'' Emma guessed. "You're probably right.''

"Thanks. That's just what I needed to hear.''

She shrugged. "You asked. I told you a long time ago that it wasn't a good idea to keep that kind of secret.''

"It's just that I was so tired of being Lauren Winters, the superstar,'' Lauren explained defensively. "Karen and I both thought it would be a good idea to leave my identity a secret at the beginning, so Wade would just be getting to know me. He didn't even know my last name until last night.''

Emma regarded her incredulously. "You were sleeping with a man who didn't know your last name?''

Lauren shrugged. "You know how it is. If you miss an introduction at the very beginning, sooner or later it begins to get awkward to ask. Besides, I was afraid it would tip him off. Turns out, he still doesn't have a clue. Now if I tell him, especially with the way he feels about money and power, I'm afraid he'll completely freak out.''

"Okay, this has gone beyond making sure that he's not just after you for your money. You have to tell him,'' Emma said flatly. In her world, things were usually black or white. It was only when it came to her sense of justice and mercy that she found the shades of gray. "The sooner, the better. I can't believe no one has slipped around him before now.''

"Probably because all of you know that I wanted to leave Hollywood behind, and people here in town have just come to accept me the way they remember me from before. They're simply relieved that I didn't come back putting on airs or dragging an entourage of celebrities with me.''

"I'm sure that's true," Emma agreed. "But you're…" She fumbled for a minute, gestured at Lauren and added, "You're *you.* How is it that no stranger has recognized you and asked for your autograph while Wade's around?''

Lauren laughed. "Not without my makeup, I'm not 'me.' Not even the tourists make the connection, though once in a long while someone will look at me with a faintly puzzled expression, as if they recognize me but can't quite place me.''

"I still say you've been lucky to get away with it this long. Tell him, Lauren, and while you're at it, explain why it was so important to you that he accept you for the woman you are. Otherwise he's going to think you deliberately set out to make a fool out of him.''

"I would never do that," Lauren protested.

"Of course you wouldn't, but he might not be able to see that if he discovers the truth some other way.''

"You're right. I know you are," Lauren said wearily. "But it's been such a relief just being me again.''

"Sweetie, being a superstar is a part of who you are. You can't lock that part of your life in a closet and forget about it. It's one of the reasons you crave your privacy, the same as me," she said with a commiserating expression. "I had my fill of media attention in Denver, and it almost destroyed me. I almost let it destroy what Ford and I were building together until I woke up and realized he was a different kind of journalist from that creep my ex-husband had bought off to ruin my professional reputation. My mistake was trying to bury the past, instead of sharing it with Ford so we could deal with it.''

Lauren was absorbing Emma's advice when Emma's cell phone rang. She still carried it out of habit, though it didn't ring nearly as persistently as it once had. Now, more often than not, it was Caitlyn calling to report on her latest riding lesson or Ford calling just to say hello. Emma fished it out of her purse, answered it, then handed it to Lauren.

''For you,'' Emma said. ''It's your agent.''

Lauren reluctantly accepted the phone. ''Jason, what on earth are you doing calling me on Emma's cell phone?''

''I called the ranch. When I told Karen it was urgent that I get in touch with you, she thought that would be the quickest way to track you down.''

''What kind of business could we possibly have that's so urgent?''

''Brace yourself,'' he warned. ''I've had a dozen inquiries in the last few days from reporters wanting to know your whereabouts.''

Lauren's heart began to thud. ''What have you told them? Why are they even looking for me?''

''I haven't told them anything,'' he said defensively. ''In fact, I've done my level best to steer them in the wrong direction, but it's possible that may have backfired.''

''Backfired how?''

''They're more determined than ever to find you. They think there's some big secret, that you're sick or locked away in drug rehab or something. One of the TV entertainment magazines got wind of the fact that you'd turned down a fortune to do that new movie. Now everybody wants to know why.''

"Oh my God," she murmured. She knew what the tabloid—and even the legitimate mainstream—reporters could be like once they sensed a big story. "Can't you issue some sort of statement?"

"I can try," Jason said. "But they're not going to rest until they see you in person. I think you should fly back, hold a press conference and dispel all the rumors. It would be better than letting them track you down, at least if you hope to maintain any privacy over there."

Lauren could see the sense in what he was suggesting, but the thought of going back, even for a day, stirred up all the tension she'd thought was finally behind her.

Then again, maybe this really would put the whole thing to rest, once and for all. No one would be able to accuse her of slipping away to hide something. And sooner or later the frenzy would die down and people would forget about her. She could live the rest of her life in blissful anonymity.

"Okay," she said at last. "I'll come back. Call my publicist and explain what's going on. Set up a press conference for tomorrow at one o'clock at your office. I'll fly in in the morning and leave right after the press conference. No one-on-one interviews."

"Great," he said. "I'll take care of it. I really do think this is for the best."

"I hope to heaven you're right," she said.

Now all she had to do was find Wade and explain everything to him before she left. He had to know the whole truth before it was splashed across the front page of every newspaper in the country. Keeping it from him now was out of the question.

When she'd hung up, she explained everything to Emma.

"You're doing the right thing," she assured Lauren. "Now get home and tell Wade." She grinned. "Maybe you can even talk him into going with you. With a man that gorgeous by your side, no one would ever question why you decided to walk away from Hollywood. Besides, everybody loves a great romance. You ought to know. You starred in enough of them."

Unfortunately, when Lauren got back to the ranch, Karen greeted her with more bad news.

"Grady and Wade had to ride up into the hills," she explained. "Some of our herd broke through a fence up there, and they're trying to round them up. I'm not expecting them back tonight. I would have gone with them, but somebody had to stay here to take care of the horses."

"That and the fact that Grady wouldn't let you go," Lauren guessed.

"Well, he did mount a pretty strenuous case against it," Karen admitted. "I decided to let him win this one, because someone did need to stay behind."

"What about me?"

"I knew the second I talked to Jason that there was a good chance you'd have to go to Los Angeles to settle this media frenzy that had him so worked up."

"That could have waited."

"No," Karen insisted. "Better to get it over with before you have photographers crawling all over Winding River. How long could it be before one of them decided to check out your hometown?"

"You're right. I'd better get upstairs and pack. Maybe I'll fly out tonight, so I'll have a little time to meet with my publicist before tomorrow's press conference. Are you sure Wade and Grady won't get back tonight?''

''Not without a miracle.''

Lauren called the local airport and made arrangements to charter the same plane she'd used before to fly her in and out of Winding River. She would call her publicist from the plane.

When she was ready to leave, she hugged Karen tightly. ''Please, whatever you do, keep Wade away from newspapers and the TV tomorrow. I have to explain all of this to him myself.''

''I'll do my best,'' Karen promised. She tucked a finger under Lauren's chin. ''Remember, chin up. Fighting spirit. And once this is over, you can put it all behind you once and for all—if that's what you want.''

''It is,'' Lauren said fervently. She just prayed it would go according to plan and that she'd still have the man she loved to come home to when it was over.

By the time Wade and Grady made it back to the ranch two days later, they were exhausted, sweaty and filthy. All Wade wanted was a long shower, some halfway decent food and a good night's sleep. A couple of sweet kisses from Lauren wouldn't be such a bad thing either, he thought with a burst of anticipation as he unsaddled his horse and headed for his house. He doubted if he could handle anything more intense right about now.

''Come on up for some food before you head to bed,'' Grady told him. ''I imagine Lauren will be around.'' He grinned. ''In case that's an incentive.''

''Oh, it is,'' Wade confirmed.

He'd actually missed her the last couple of days.

Never before, with the exception of his mother, had he had ties to anyone that ran deep enough for him to care whether he saw them from one minute to the next or not. Phone calls satisfied his need to be in touch with his mother, but that wouldn't be nearly enough with Lauren. In fact, now he knew with certainty that he couldn't go for long without catching a glimpse of her, without holding her in his arms.

He rushed through his shower, pulled on clean clothes and hurried up to the main house. Karen greeted him with a smile.

"You must be starved. I've got breakfast almost ready. Have a seat. Grady should be back down any minute."

He glanced around, but there was no sign of Lauren. "Where's Lauren?" he asked, not giving two hoots if he appeared overly anxious. Everyone in this house seemed to know where things stood between them anyway.

A flash of something that might have been guilt tracked across Karen's face. "She had to go out of town unexpectedly."

Wade's gut began to churn. "When?"

"The same day you and Grady took off to round up the cattle."

"Where'd she go?"

"Los Angeles. She thought she'd be back yesterday, but she got held up. She called last night. She expects to be home by tonight."

Thoughts of that persistent business associate of hers tormented him. "Does this have something to do with Jason?" he asked, his voice tight.

Karen kept her back to him, deliberately focusing on the bacon she was cooking. "I'll let her explain everything. She'd hoped to talk to you last night. She was disappointed that you weren't home yet.''

Wade shoved away from the table, his appetite suddenly gone. ''Thanks for the offer of breakfast, but I've got to go.''

She turned then, her expression stricken. ''Don't go. The food's ready.''

''No appetite,'' he insisted. ''I need sleep more than I need food.''

All the way to his place, he wrestled with his rude behavior and the reason for it. He had no business taking it out on Karen just because he was disappointed— okay, upset—by Lauren's vanishing act the minute his back was turned. He was just exhausted. That had to be it. He trusted Lauren, didn't he? Of course he did. She had never given him any reason to do otherwise. She had explained about this Jason person time and again. There was no reason to be worried.

In fact, the way to avoid this kind of response in the future was to solidify their relationship. It was all well and good to say that they were committed to each other, as they had the other night, but marriage was the only commitment that really counted.

With that thought in mind, Wade managed to catch a couple of hours of sleep, then drove to Laramie in search of a jewelry store. He was going to do this right. He'd buy Lauren the most expensive ring he could afford, maybe get some flowers and a bottle of champagne and be ready and waiting for her when she got home from this trip.

Once they were married, he'd never have to doubt what they'd found with each other again. She could take off and go around the world on a whim, but he'd know that she was always going to come home to him.

He honestly didn't know how he'd gotten to be so lucky. He'd never expected to meet a woman who was not only gorgeous, but who knew horses the way Lauren did, a woman who wouldn't mind sharing the hard work of ranch life. He was beginning to believe in that destiny stuff people talked about. He and Lauren could build a good future together.

He couldn't give her everything she deserved overnight, but he'd been putting money aside. He could buy his own spread in another year or two. The breeding was already coming along, thanks to his partnership with Grady. They were already on their way to having some of the best stock in Wyoming. Until all the pieces fell into place, he could go on working for Grady. Lauren could, too, if that's what she wanted. Or she could hire out to other ranchers, consult with them on horses that needed someone to take a little extra time, use a little extra ingenuity in their training.

Or she could just stay at home and have their babies. The thought brought an unexpected swell of feeling up from deep inside him. Wade had never imagined wanting a family so much, never thought about being a husband, much less a father. But seeing the tenderness between Karen and Grady now that she was carrying his child had made him want that for himself. He'd wanted to watch Lauren grow big with his baby inside her.

Because he wanted all of it so badly, he should have known it was destined to blow up in his face. That was the way things went in his life. Nothing was ever as perfect as it seemed. Nothing lasted.

As he stood in a Laramie drugstore, frozen in place, his gaze locked on the front page of a tabloid, his entire world came crashing down just when he was beginning to think it was perfect.

There was no mistaking that incredible face, no mistaking the dazzling smile, though the rest—the glamorous hairdo, the jewels, the designer gown—were as unfamiliar to him as pricey champagne.

Why Is This Superstar Hiding Out? the headline asked.

Wade stared at the picture, dumbfounded. For a second, he dared to hope that it was her twin, but there was her name beneath the picture, the full name she had deliberately kept from him for months, the name she had been so reluctant to share even when he'd pushed.

In a daze, he picked up the paper and carried it out to his truck. He sat in the front seat, the paper resting on the steering wheel, the damning words swimming in front of eyes that were blurry with unshed tears.

Again and again, his gaze was drawn back to the expensive beaded gown that must have cost more than his annual salary. Lauren's hair, which fell over him in a shower of fire when they made love, was done up on top of her head with glittering jewels tucked among the curls. Diamonds, no doubt. His stomach clenched at the sight.

All these months and he hadn't known—hadn't even guessed—that she had this other life. All these months she had been lying to him, making a fool of him. She was everything he hated—wealthy, powerful, duplicitous, conniving. How could he not have known that about her? How could he have let himself be deceived the same way his mother had been? Only this was worse, because Lauren had known how he felt about all the things she apparently was. She had known and played with his emotions anyway.

And what about Grady? Why hadn't he said something? He knew Wade was falling for Lauren. He'd even encouraged it. All of them had. But Grady was his friend, or so he'd thought. Why hadn't he warned Wade off, told him she was out of his league?

He balled up the paper and tossed it on the seat beside him. Filled with gut-churning outrage and betrayal, he drove back to the ranch, packed his things, tossed them haphazardly into the back of his truck, and went to look for Grady.

"I just wanted you to know I'm taking off," he said tightly when he found Grady. "I figured I owed you that courtesy, which is a helluva lot more than I got from you."

Grady regarded him with a shocked expression. "What's that supposed to mean? What's gotten into you?"

"You and your wife and your superstar friend must have been having a great time laughing behind my back," Wade said, tossing the crumpled newspaper down in front of Grady. He gestured toward the picture of Lauren. "What was I? Some brief interlude with the hired help that Lauren could brag about when she went back to her fancy digs in California?"

"I don't know what you're talking about," Grady insisted.

Wade regarded his boss incredulously. "You didn't know that Lauren is a big-time Hollywood actress?"

"Of course I knew that." Grady's jaw dropped. "Didn't you?"

"How would I know?"

"The whole town knows who Lauren is. I figured you'd heard about her. And since you've gotten closer, what you didn't hear I figured she'd tell you herself. I know she's been hoping to maintain a low profile now that she's back, but of all people I thought she'd want you to know."

Wade regarded him with a wry look. "Yeah, you would think that, wouldn't you? Well, she didn't."

"Wade, don't leave," Grady pleaded. "Think about this. There has to be some sort of misunderstanding. I know how she feels about you. She loves you. She'll be back any time now. She called Karen from the airport in Los Angeles just as she was taking off."

A part of Wade wanted to believe Grady, wanted to believe that his own instincts hadn't failed him completely, but the truth was staring him square in the face. Lauren Winters had lied to him, just like every other person with money he'd ever known, starting with the rich daddy who hadn't seen fit to claim a bastard son.

This hurt worse, though, because he'd never expected anything from his father, not even acknowledgment. But he'd started to expect a lot from Lauren. He'd started to count on a future.

When he thought of the ring he'd almost bought, with its tiny, glittering diamond that would have been a joke compared to the ones she'd worn in her hair in that picture, he wanted to break things.

But losing his temper would solve nothing. It would only tell Grady just how deeply he'd been hurt, and he'd thrown his pride out the window for way too long now. Right about now, it was all he had left to cling to.

"Just tell her I couldn't stick around for more of her lies," he told Grady.

"What about the horses?" Grady asked, clearly looking for any excuse to stall him. "You have a right to part of our stock. Give it a day or two, and we can work something out that's fair."

"I don't want anything from this place. I'll take Miss Molly with me, but the rest are yours. When I get settled, you can send me a check."

"Wade, please. Think this over. See Lauren when she gets back. You can work it out. I know you can."

Wade didn't think he could bear ever to set eyes on her again. He just shook his head, turned his back and walked away. He couldn't put Lauren Winters and the Blackhawk ranch behind him fast enough to suit him. He'd been right all along. He just wasn't cut out for any kind of permanence. He'd been a fool to think otherwise.

Chapter Fourteen

It had been the trip from hell. Jason had been right about one thing—the entertainment media was in a frenzy. What he'd been totally mistaken about was any possibility that one little press conference would satisfy them.

Someone had found out Lauren was flying in by chartered jet. There had been a horde of reporters waiting for her at the airport. Refusing to comment, she'd forced her way through the crowd to the limo Jason had sent.

Relieved by the narrow escape, she hadn't been prepared for yet another throng of cameras and microphones at the gate to her secluded house high above Beverly Hills. She hadn't thought to call the security company and request extra guards. It took two endless hours for them to send reinforcements who could chase away the reporters who'd managed to slip onto the property.

By that night she felt as if she was under siege. The phone never stopped ringing. The guards had been ordered not to even bother calling from the gatehouse. She was seeing no one, she told them firmly.

She had checked in with Karen that night and again in the morning before leaving for Jason's office, but there had been no sign of Wade back at the ranch at that point. Nor had he returned by the time the nerve-racking press conference had ended. Lauren could really have used a comforting word about then, something to remind her of what was waiting for her back in Wyoming.

Because no one was satisfied that they'd gotten the whole story at the press conference, there were a dozen demanding requests for further interviews. Jason and her publicist tried to fend them off but eventually warned her that if she didn't agree, the reporters were entirely likely to follow her back to Winding River now that they were on the scent of a hot story.

Back in the agency conference room the next day, she had endured the same questions over and over, in interview after interview until she'd thought she might scream. The only thing that had kept her going was an image of Wade firmly planted in her mind, though she was increasingly frustrated by her inability to catch up with him.

Worse, on the flight home, when she'd called yet again hoping to connect with him, Karen had been amazingly tight-lipped regarding his whereabouts. Something was wrong, terribly wrong. She could feel it.

"Tell me what's happened," she'd pleaded to no avail. "Is he hurt?"

"No, not physically," Karen had said cryptically.

"What does that mean?"

"We'll talk about it when you get here. Grady and I will pick you up."

That should have been her clue that things had gone dreadfully awry. Why hadn't Wade been the one to come to pick her up? Wasn't he as anxious to see her as she was to see him?

Now she was sitting in the kitchen at the ranch with Karen fussing over a pot of tea and Grady looking as if he'd rather be anywhere else on earth.

"Okay, that's it," Lauren finally snapped. "What's going on? Where *is* Wade? And why are you both acting as if there's going to be a funeral?"

Karen carefully placed a cup of tea in front of her, then rested a hand on her shoulder. "Sweetie, Wade's gone."

For one horrible, terrifying second Lauren thought she meant forever, as in dead, as in some awful accident or heart attack. "Not dead," she whispered when she could squeeze the word past the terror lodged in her throat.

Karen looked stricken. "Oh, God, no. I'm sorry. Of all people, I should know to be more careful about choosing my words in a situation like this. Everyone was so careful when Caleb died, tiptoeing around the truth. This isn't the same at all. I meant that Wade has left."

Even with the clarification, Lauren didn't understand, wouldn't *let* herself understand.

"He's gone?" Fighting shock, Lauren tore her gaze from Karen and stared at Grady. "But why? Where would he go?'' When no answers were forthcoming, her voice faltered. "He's really gone? You're sure?"

Grady's expression was full of pity. It was almost more than Lauren could bear. He nodded.

"I'm sorry," he told her. "I watched him pack up his truck and leave. I tried to stop him. Believe me, the last thing I wanted was to see him take off like that, but he wouldn't listen to reason. Nothing I said could persuade him to stick around till you got back."

"But it's just for a few days, right? A sudden trip, like mine? Maybe something happened to his mother, an emergency of some kind," she said, clinging to hope by a thread, refusing to believe the obvious conclusion to be drawn from the fact that Wade had packed his belongings into his truck before he'd driven off.

"He took Miss Molly," Grady said, clearly knowing that that was the most telling indicator of Wade's intentions.

Lauren struggled with the implications. "But why?" she asked, even though the answer was staring her in the face. There was a newspaper lying right there on the kitchen table, a paper that had plainly been twisted by someone filled with anger. Lauren spread it out on the table, smoothed the front page, then gasped. It was the first time she'd seen how the story of her disappearance had been played out by the media. This one had been written before the press conference, and it was filled with innuendo and speculation, most of it damning. But the mere existence of her picture on the front page had no doubt been more than enough to cause Wade to bolt straight out of her life. It was what Emma had predicted. He felt utterly betrayed.

"Oh my God," she whispered, imagining all that

must have gone through Wade's mind when he'd seen it.

"What?" Karen demanded, then peered over her shoulder. "Oh, hell."

Grady nodded. "That about sums it up. Wade wasn't real happy about being deceived. Lauren, I love you like a sister, but what were you thinking?"

Karen groaned. "This is all my fault, Lauren. I'm the one who told you not to tell him what you did for a living."

Grady stared at her, his expression incredulous. "You? Why? Honesty has always been such a huge thing with you."

Karen regarded him with an impatient expression. "Oh, you know perfectly well why. I thought it would give them a chance to get to know each other without all the rest getting in the way. It wasn't a lie, just an omission," she snapped, then sighed. "It was a mistake. I can see that now."

Lauren knew that all the blame didn't belong with her friend. She had to accept the bulk of it. She'd been so happy knowing that Wade really cared for *her,* not some mythical superstar who didn't really exist, that she'd let the masquerade go on way too long. She and Emma had talked about that very thing. She had resolved to tell Wade everything just when things had started to spin out of control in California.

Of course, there had been a hundred times before that when she should have told Wade the truth, when she should have shared the last ten years of her life with him. Instead, she had kept it a secret as if it was something of which she was ashamed. No wonder he felt betrayed.

She had to make him see why she'd done it, had to

tell him that she was in love with him, had to convince him to forgive her. But how could she when she had no idea where he was?

"I have to find him," she told her friends. "I have to make things right."

"And then what?" Grady asked. "Are you saying you have no intention of going back to Hollywood, of picking up where you left off? Wade will never be happy out there."

"Grady's right," Karen said. "Be sure of exactly what you want before you go after him."

For once in her life, Lauren did know what she wanted. She was surprised that it wasn't plain to Karen, who knew her as well as anyone on earth did.

"I thought you knew," she said to her best friend. "I want this. What you two have. Isn't that obvious? If it isn't clear to *you,* it's little wonder that Wade didn't get it."

Karen regarded her with an unwavering stare. "Then why haven't you sold your house in Los Angeles? For that matter, why are you still living here with us?"

Lauren flinched at the question. Hurt and flustered, she simply stared back. "I..."

Instantly apologetic, Karen reached for her hand and gave it a squeeze. "Sweetie, I am not asking that to hurt your feelings or to suggest for one single minute that you're not welcome here. I'm just saying that anyone looking at this situation—even me—has to wonder if it's not temporary. That house in California, Jason's constant calls—it looks to an outsider as if you're hedging your bets."

In fact, there was a picture of that very house accompanying the article that began on the tabloid's front page and filled two more pages inside. Wade must have looked at it and thought the same thing that Karen was daring to say. With all of that waiting for her in California, why would she ever consider a life with a man who lived in a cottage on another man's land?

"Oh, God, what have I done?" she asked with a moan.

"Nothing that can't be fixed," Karen said optimistically. "If you're sure about what you really want."

"I'm sure," Lauren insisted. She wanted the life she'd had the last couple of months with Wade. She wanted kids and a ranch and friends she could count on. It was so much more than she'd ever found as a celebrity.

But how could she make him believe that, how could she make him see that the life she'd left behind, the one she'd hidden from him, meant nothing to her?

Words wouldn't do it with him any more than they had with Jason. Nor could she count on empty promises. She needed a grand gesture. Something he would see as irrefutable evidence of her intentions.

And she was pretty sure she knew exactly what it should be. She looked across the table at Grady and Karen.

"Is the Grigsby ranch still for sale?" she asked, knowing that Otis Junior had been anxious to get whatever he could for it at the same time he'd sold off the horses. She feared he might have found a buyer just as eager to steal the property from someone to whom it only represented a leftover nuisance from a life he'd long ago abandoned.

Her friends exchanged a look, then nodded.

"How about Midnight?" she asked. "Would you sell him to me?"

A grin spread across Karen's face. "Absolutely."

"Hey, wait a minute," Grady protested. "That horse—"

His wife cut him off. "That horse is Lauren's wedding gift to Wade. Am I right?"

Lauren nodded. "If he'll have us."

Grady frowned at his wife. "I was just going to say that Wade already owns half of that horse."

"All the better," Lauren said, warming to her plan. "Then if I buy your half stake in him, we'll be joint owners."

"Say yes, Grady," Karen prodded.

Grady gave both of them a resigned look. "Fine. Yes. Midnight is all yours. Yours and Wade's, that is. He's going to be expecting a check, though. I told him I'd find a buyer for Midnight and the other horses and send him his share of the proceeds."

Lauren reached for her checkbook. "How much?"

Karen gasped. "You don't want him to find out that you've bought them, do you?"

"No, the check will be to Grady. He can pay Wade. Full value, too. I don't want any deals."

Grady's eyes lit up with feigned avarice. "Now that's what I like to hear," he teased. "Of course, if you make that check too big, Wade might not have any incentive to come back."

"Grady!" Karen protested.

"Except to see Lauren, of course," he added hurriedly.

"I knew what you meant," Lauren assured him. "How much?"

He named a figure she knew to be reasonable given the quality of the stock she was buying. She ripped the check out and handed it to him.

"Now all I have to do is buy someplace to keep them," she said wearily.

"Not until morning," Karen said emphatically. "We all need a good night's sleep."

"Especially you, little mama," Grady said, his gaze suddenly tender.

"Oh my gosh, I forgot about the baby," Lauren said with dismay. "Go up to bed right now. You need all the rest you can get."

Karen scowled at her. "Don't you start, too. One worrywart in the house is enough. I'm getting plenty of sleep. Lauren's the one who looks as if she's been run over by a truck."

"Thanks so much," Lauren mocked. "But I'm too wound up to sleep yet. Go on to bed. I'll clean up the dishes before I come up."

"It's three teacups," Karen countered. "Leave them."

"It will take me five seconds. Now scoot, you two."

After they'd gone, Lauren washed the cups, then went onto the porch. It was a clear, starry night with just a hint of fall in the air.

Too restless to sit and enjoy it, she set out on a walk. The moon was bright enough to light the way. She went first to the barn to look in on Midnight. The horse's ears pricked up the instant she came near.

"Hi, big fellow. Did you miss me?"

He nudged her pockets in search of sugar or carrots.

"Sorry. I forgot."

As if he understood and forgave her, he simply nudged her again, his big eyes soulful.

"What am I going to do if this plan doesn't work?" she asked him, sliding her arms around his neck and resting her head against him. Midnight tolerated the gesture, whinnying softly in response.

She drew in a deep breath, relishing the scents of horses and fresh hay and oats. No negative thoughts, she admonished herself. Her plan *was* going to work. It had to. Her entire future depended on it.

The Grigsby ranch was a disaster, even worse than Lauren had remembered. The Calamity Janes wandered through the empty house with her, clucking under their breath and muttering their certainty that Lauren had finally lost her mind completely.

"Okay, just spit it out," she said finally. "What are the big objections?"

"It's falling down," Cassie said at once.

"The kitchen hasn't been renovated since the Dark Ages," Gina said, predictably fixated on the ancient appliances.

"It will cost a fortune to heat, unless you spend a fortune making it more airtight than it is right now," Emma said, shuddering. "I can feel a breeze standing right here. In another month or so this place will be freezing."

"Maybe you're feeling a breeze because the window is open," Lauren suggested optimistically.

"Nope, the air is coming up through the floor," Emma retorted, then latched onto Karen's arm. "Stand here. Is that air or not?"

Karen stood silently where she'd been directed, then nodded. "It's definitely air." She turned to Lauren. "Sorry. I cannot lie to a member of the legal profession."

Lauren shrugged off the problem. "I don't care. I want it. It's the best piece of property available."

"How do you know?"

"Because I called the real estate agent first thing this morning and asked about all the listings in the area before I arranged to pick up the keys to see this one," she said. "Trust me, if I want a ranch nearby, this is the cream of the crop."

"It's a knockdown," Cassie said, her expression dire. "You'd have to start from scratch. Do you want to spend that much time and money on this?"

Since Lauren had no firm idea where Wade was or when Grady might hear from him, she had all the time in the world. "Yes," she said very firmly, then one by one looked each of them squarely in the eye to emphasize the point. "And I'm not tearing it down. I'll renovate it. It'll be the first good use I've had for my money in a long time."

"Okay, then," Emma said briskly. "I'll do the negotiating. Otis Junior is slime. It will be a pleasure taking him to the cleaners."

"The money goes to Otis Senior," Lauren reminded her. "He's up in years and not all that well. He might need it for his care."

"Good point," Cassie chimed in.

"Then I'll have to insist it be put in a trust for just that, so that Otis Junior can't touch it while his daddy's alive," Emma said, pulling her cell phone from her purse to call the real estate agent.

While Emma and the agent negotiated, the others kept on wandering around making notes on all that needed to be done. They came back eventually and handed several sheets of paper to Lauren.

"Just a few starting points," Gina said with a grin. "I put the kitchen on top. I can't be expected to cook dinners for all of us in the state it's in now."

Lauren gave her an impulsive hug. "Thank you."

"For what?"

"For seeing the potential."

"Oh, I'm not sure I'd go that far," Gina said. "But there's nothing I like better than designing the way a kitchen ought to look so that it functions efficiently."

Lauren glanced at the sketch she'd drawn. "Isn't this a little big?"

"I figure you won't really want a formal dining room. I think having a big, friendly kitchen where all your friends and family can gather is much cozier, don't you?"

Lauren chuckled. "Why do I get the feeling this is your dream kitchen, not mine?"

"There's no reason it can't be yours," Gina retorted. "Besides, Rafe says I have a perfectly good kitchen at Tony's. He doesn't see why I need another one at home since we never eat there. So, here you go, this is the one I'd have if he weren't so mule-headed. It's all yours. Consider it your housewarming present."

"There's just one thing you're not taking into account," Lauren pointed out. "I can't cook, nothing beyond the basics, anyway."

Gina stared at her, clearly horrified. "How did I let that happen? We'll start with cooking lessons tomorrow. You can't expect the man to marry you if you can't even put an interesting meal on the table."

"Believe me, my problems with Wade run far deeper than whether I can make a decent casserole," Lauren said.

"Well, we have to start somewhere," Gina told her just as Emma hung up, her expression triumphant.

"It's yours," she said. "We got a good deal and

protected Otis Senior. All in all, a terrific negotiation, if I do say so myself.''

''Emma, you're magnificent,'' Lauren praised.

''Well, of course she is,'' Cassie said, grinning at her. ''She's one of us.''

''Look what I found,'' Gina said, emerging from another foray into the kitchen with five paper cups filled with tap water. ''We can have a toast to your new home.''

They lifted the cups into the air and Karen said, ''To Lauren. May she find the same kind of happiness here that the rest of us have found, and may it last forever.''

''To Lauren,'' the others chorused.

Tears welled up in Lauren's eyes as she looked around her. She had a house. She had her friends. Now if only she could get Wade to come back, she would have everything any woman could possibly want.

''Oh, no,'' Cassie murmured. ''She's crying.''

''I am not,'' Lauren said.

''She's just realized what she's done,'' Emma said. ''I can always call and say the deal's off.''

''Don't you dare. This is exactly what I want.''

''A falling-down house?'' Emma said skeptically. ''It's not too late. I can get you out of it. There's a grace period for buyer's remorse.''

''Absolutely not. I want a home where I can build a family, and this is it.'' Her voice quivered slightly. ''There's just one thing missing.''

''If Wade Owens has an ounce of sense in his head, he'll be back,'' Karen assured her. ''In the meantime, there is a lot of work to be done if this place is going to be ready to welcome him.''

''Tomorrow's Saturday,'' Gina pointed out. ''I can

spare a few hours in the morning. So can Rafe. What about the rest of you?''

"Cole and I will be here," Cassie promised.

"And Grady and I," Karen added. "Though he'll probably insist I sit in a corner and watch all the activity."

"I'll be here, but I'm not sure I trust Ford on any ladders," Emma said. "It's not that he's clumsy, but he gets some idea in his head for a story and he gets distracted."

Funny, Lauren thought as she fought off more tears. Compared to her place in California, this place truly was a disaster. It didn't even have any real charm on its side. But despite that, it still felt more like a home than any place she'd ever lived.

Or it would once Wade stepped through the door and declared that he was back in her life to stay.

Chapter Fifteen

Wade hadn't intended to go back to Winding River, not ever. The memories there were too painful. The prospect of bumping into Lauren was even worse. When he thought of how she had deceived him, it made him physically ill. When he thought of how desperately he loved her just the same, it made him curse the day they'd crossed paths.

For the first couple of months after he'd left, he bummed around the rodeo circuit, caring for stock, looking for…something. Work, maybe. A stud he could build his ranch around one day, one with half the spirit and bloodlines of Midnight. A pair of green eyes that could dazzle him or a soft body that would fit his as perfectly as the one he'd left behind.

He found none of that. In fact, his head was filled with memories of Winding River and a woman who'd given him something he'd never expected to find, then ruined it all by betraying him.

When the memory of her face began to dim, he found himself in a video store, searching for all her old movies. He wanted to see for himself the woman she'd kept from him. Watching her face light up the screen, listening to her voice, he'd been as captivated as he'd once been by the real woman. It was little wonder that she had legions of fans, little wonder that she hadn't been able to turn her back on all of that for the life he could have offered her.

Not that he'd given her a chance to say no, he admitted grudgingly. Because he'd known what the answer would be. No way could what he was offering stack up to the millions she was making in Hollywood or the adoration of thousands of fans. He had a hard time admitting it was pride that had made him leave town without confronting her, but that was the truth of the matter. The pitiful fact was that he would have forgiven her betrayal in a heartbeat if he'd thought for one single second that they stood even a small chance of making it.

When the phone in his cheap motel room rang, he stared at it. "What the hell?" No one knew where he was. No one who mattered, anyway. With the kind of pickup work he was doing these days, he answered to no one. Nobody kept track of his whereabouts.

His mental dismissal didn't seem to stop the ringing. It went on and on until he finally yanked up the receiver just to stop the noise.

"Yeah, what?"

"Gracious as ever, I see," Grady Blackhawk said.

Wade was stunned. He'd deliberately not gotten in touch with Grady because he'd feared the other man would reveal his location to Lauren. Stubborn as she was, she might come after him out of some sense of obligation, and he knew that he didn't have the strength to resist her if she did. Maybe in a few months he would, but not yet.

"What the hell do you want?" he asked curtly.

"I want you to come back."

"Not an option," Wade said.

"Lauren's gone."

"So what?" he asked, though for some reason his heart ached at the news. She had gone back to Hollywood, after all, just as he'd predicted.

It didn't surprise him. That sudden trip she'd taken to Los Angeles had clearly been the handwriting on the wall. The lark was over. Once she was back in the spotlight, evidently she'd decided it suited her better than a ranch in Wyoming.

"Thought it might make it easier for you to say yes, if you knew that," Grady said, as if he'd been dangling a tasty carrot in front of Midnight.

"It doesn't matter," Wade lied.

"Can't face the memories?" Grady inquired, hitting the nail on the head. "Maybe that should tell you something."

"All it tells me is that I made the worst mistake of my life when I thought I'd be enough for her. In fact, she's probably enjoying herself back in Hollywood now, laughing over her brief romance with a small-town cowboy. It'll make a great anecdote for her next TV interview."

He'd caught one of those interviews on the night he'd first left town. She'd looked so gorgeous, so composed and glamorous, he'd simply stared at the screen, fascinated and sick at heart.

"Lauren would never demean what the two of you shared that way," Grady chided. "And if you weren't being an idiot, you'd know that. She loved you."

"Let's not even go there," Wade warned. "If I'm even going to consider what you're asking, we have to agree that the topic of Lauren is off limits."

"Fine. Whatever," Grady retorted. "Just don't let your damn stubbornness and pride keep you from doing what you know you want to do. I've got a job with your name on it. Come back, Wade."

Then the sneaky, conniving, son of a bitch added, "The baby's due soon. We really need all the extra help around here we can get."

Wade felt the knot in his stomach ease. He'd been looking forward to the baby's arrival almost as much as Grady and his grandfather, Thomas Blackhawk, had. The news had been a turning point for Wade. It had kicked off the start of his own dreams for the future.

"Your grandfather must be over the moon by now. Is he driving you crazy?" he asked.

"He's been hovering the last couple of weeks. He thinks the whole thing was all his idea. I might have to fight him to get to be in the delivery room," Grady confirmed. "So, anyway, you can see that Karen's going to be out of commission for a while. Help me out."

Grady was right, Wade thought. Why shouldn't he go back if Lauren wasn't there? She probably wouldn't show her face until the next class reunion in another eight or nine years, and by then surely his heart would be completely healed. Working for Grady had been the best setup he'd ever had even before Lauren had set foot on the ranch. Why should he sacrifice that just because the fool woman had broken his heart?

"Will Karen be able to keep her nose out of this? I don't want her pestering me about Lauren."

"She won't say a word," Grady promised.

"I'll believe that when I see it." Wade uttered a little sigh of resignation. "I'll be there as soon as I can get there." He paused, suddenly thoughtful. "How did you find me, anyway?"

"Does it matter?" Grady asked, sounding evasive. "All that counts is the fact that you're coming back where you belong."

Yeah, maybe. But it remained to be seen if he could bear being there without Lauren.

Wade had been back for two weeks now, and aside from enduring speculative looks from both Grady and Karen, it hadn't been so bad. Images of Lauren only popped into his head every hour or so.

He'd been stunned to discover that Grady had sold Midnight and their other horses, but he'd explained that the new owner had made him an offer too good to turn down. And without Wade or Lauren there to train the still-fractious stallion, Grady had seen no point in holding out. He'd handed Wade a sizable check for his share and assured him they could start looking for a new stallion and some broodmares whenever Wade was ready.

"It could be a while," Wade told him. He just didn't have the heart for it right now. That dream and marrying Lauren had gotten all twisted up together in his head. It was too soon to consider following through with one without having the other.

Grady frowned at the response. "Why wait? At least take a ride over to the Grigsby place this morning," he suggested over breakfast. "There's a horse over there I'd like you to take a look at. He sounds too good to pass up.''

''What's the rush?'' Wade asked, regarding him with puzzlement. ''You obviously weren't that anxious to have a horse operation, or you wouldn't have sold off our stock. You know perfectly well you could have found another wrangler to replace me.''

''Didn't see much point to keeping it without you around to manage things. I've got enough irons in the fire,'' Grady insisted. ''Now that you're back, things are different. Besides, from what I hear, they won't have that horse long. Somebody's going to come along and snap it up. You'll be kicking yourself if it's not you.''

''I don't see why you're pushing so hard, but I'll drive over later and check him out,'' Wade promised, then glanced curiously at Karen. It had almost sounded as if she'd uttered a sigh of relief. Or maybe it had just been a plain old sigh. She was pretty far along in the pregnancy now, and all her movements seemed to be a struggle. That must have been it, he concluded, then turned back to Grady.

''I thought that ranch was up for sale back when we bought that stock. Did Otis or that son of his decide against it?''

''No, it sold,'' Grady told him. ''The new owner's starting up a horse ranch. There's some fine stock over there already. Now that you've got that check in hand, I thought you ought to go over and take a look, just see what's available.''

''Okay, okay, I said I would.'' Caving in to the pressure, Wade grabbed his hat and headed for the door, then glanced back at Karen, who was watching him intently. "You're not going to deliver that baby today, are you?"

She looked startled by the question. "No, why?"

"You seem a little jumpy, and I heard that sigh a bit ago. If you were having pains or anything, you'd tell Grady, right?"

"Of course I would," she insisted.

"She'd better," Grady said, his expression dire.

"Okay then," Wade said. "I'll head on over to the Grigsby place. Do you know the new owner's name?"

"No," they chorused so emphatically that it stirred his suspicions at once.

"Haven't met 'em yet," Karen said, then patted her swollen belly. "I haven't been getting out and about the last few weeks. I'll be anxious to hear all about them and what they've done with the place."

Wade grinned at her. "Then I'll be sure to take notes on the paint and the curtains. Anything else in particular you'd like to know?"

"Oh, just what you think of them," she said.

He nodded. "I'll report in the minute I get back," he promised, chuckling over her blatant curiosity. Nosy as she was, he could imagine how frustrating it must be for her not to have been over to check things out for herself.

An hour later Wade pulled into the winding driveway of the newly named L&W Ranch. He could see a few of the improvements right off. New fences had gone up. The pasture was greener. And there were indeed some fine-looking horses.

The house itself had been painted, yellow with white shutters and white trim on the porch. A couple of comfortable-looking rockers sat side by side with a good view of the pastures. Whoever had bought the place had put some money into it, no doubt about it. It would be a fine place for a family. A part of him regretted that he wouldn't be the one living there. The potential he'd seen back a few months when he and Lauren had come for the horse auction had been fulfilled.

When he rounded the house, parked and stepped out of his truck, the first thing he noticed was that the horse in the corral was Midnight. There was no mistaking the sleek animal. Nor was there any mistake about the woman who was about to get into the saddle on his back. His heart leaped into his throat, quickly followed by panic. The latter overrode his dismay.

He was about to bolt in their direction, but Midnight stood perfectly still, clearly unfazed by his rider. Lauren leaned down to whisper in the horse's ear. As if he understood her perfectly, he whinnied a response. Lauren laughed and caressed his neck. Just as he had months ago, Wade shuddered with envy at that touch. What kind of fool did that make him? He was still jealous of a horse, and all over a woman who'd betrayed him and no doubt hadn't given him a second thought since.

Lauren glanced over at him then, her expression solemn. "Welcome home."

He had the distinct impression that she was referring to more than his return to Winding River.

"Care to go for a ride?" she asked.

Wade didn't know what to say, didn't know what to make of her presence here, of her attitude, of the sneaky way Grady had gotten him over here…of anything. This Lauren wasn't the superstar he'd seen weeks ago in that tabloid or on the color TV in his motel room. This was the down-to-earth woman he loved with everything in him. What was the use of trying to deny it? If the depth of that love hadn't changed in all this time, it wasn't going to.

But because he wasn't going to risk his heart a second time, he settled for asking, "Why are you here?"

"I own the place. Well, I'm half owner of it, actually. The other owner's been away."

His gaze narrowed and his heart began its own little two-step. "Is that so?"

"I'm hoping he might be back to stay now," she said, her gaze on his, her expression uncertain. "Is he?"

His hands bunched into fists. He jammed them into his pockets to keep from reaching for her. "What are you saying, Lauren?"

"That this ranch is half yours," she said as casually as if she were announcing that she'd bought him a new CD by his favorite country singer.

"Why?"

"Because it seems to me a deed ought to be in the names of both the husband and the wife, so there's no mistaking that it's jointly owned." She frowned. "You did see the gate, didn't you? It's the L&W Ranch now."

As the absurd scope of the gesture sank in, he simply stared at her. "You bought me a ranch?" he repeated incredulously.

"I bought *us* a ranch," she corrected, grinning. "What do you think?"

"If this is some sort of act, you're very convincing."

"I've been told that before, but maybe we ought to leave my acting skills out of this. That's what got us into trouble before." She dismounted and walked over to him. "So, what do you say, cowboy? Will you marry me?"

"Hold it. I'm having a hard time putting this all together. You intend to stay right here?"

"Yep."

"What about your career?"

"This is my career now. It's the only one I want."

She sounded very convincing, but he was still afraid to believe his good fortune, terrified to believe that she would choose him over her career. "You'll be content to be a rancher's wife?" he asked doubtfully.

"Absolutely," she said without hesitation. "I'd already made that choice before you and I ever met. I wasn't here on some lark back then, Wade. I'd come home. You made me certain I'd done the right thing."

"But the excitement, the glamour, the money," he said. "How can you turn your back on all of that?"

"It was a fluke," she said. "I'll tell you all about it if you want to know, but for now you just need to understand that I never wanted any of it. Oh, it was fun for a while and I got caught up in it, but *this* life is *real*. The people here are real." Her gaze clashed with his. "And the man I love is here...and he's real."

He searched her face for even the tiniest hint that she was lying to him, but her expression was open and sincere. He wanted to believe her. God, how he wanted to believe her.

She touched his cheek. "The only question is, can you live with being labeled the superstar's cowboy in every tabloid coast to coast? It will come to that. I can almost guarantee it."

Wade thought about it, thought about learning to live with who Lauren Winters really was. And then it came to him, *this* was who she was, this sexy woman who knew horses, loved the outdoors and loved him. He'd never even met that other Lauren Winters, though in the past weeks he'd watched every movie she'd ever made two and three times. They had made him heartsick over what he'd lost. He'd realized she was good on-screen, so he knew now what she was willing to give up to be with him. The most amazing part of all was that she apparently didn't consider it any sort of sacrifice. In fact, if she was being totally honest here, she seemed to think it was a more-than-even trade.

"What if I said no?" he asked carefully. "Would you still stay on here?"

Her eyes locked with his. "Yes," she said quietly. "But I would miss you every single day of my life."

The words settled over Wade like a benediction, chasing away the last of his doubts, promising him everything he'd ever dreamed of.

"Okay, then," he said, the beginnings of a smile tugging at his lips. "I'll marry you on one condition." As if her agreement were a certainty, he was already reaching for her.

"What's that?"

"Promise to take me to the Academy Awards one of these days, just so we can tell our kids we've been."

She leaped into his arms and covered his face with kisses. "We'll ride in on a pair of white horses," she promised. "They'll be talking about it for years to come."

He laughed, suddenly feeling as giddy as if he'd been granted the moon and stars. He twirled her around until they were both dizzy, but then his mood sobered as reality crept in.

"Will you be content, Lauren? Can you be satisfied not being a somebody?"

She frowned at him. "Don't you ever say that, Wade Owens. I *will* be a somebody. I will be a rancher and a mother and, best of all, I'll be your wife."

Wade nodded thoughtfully, then swept her up and kissed her soundly. "Then I don't give two hoots what the tabloids call me, darlin', because you and I are getting hitched."

"Thank goodness," she teased. "For a minute there, you had me worried."

"No need to worry. You're not the only one in the family with a flair for the dramatic. I know a happy ending when I see one." He grinned. "In fact, it reminds me a little bit of *Kiss the Stars.*"

She looked surprised at that. "You saw that? When?"

"The better question might be how many times?" he admitted. "Probably a half-dozen. I think it was my favorite."

"Mine, too," she said. "The critics hated it. They thought it was sappy."

Wade met her gaze. "What do they know? They're just frustrated screenwriters who are jealous of a good thing."

Lauren laughed. "When did you get to be so smart?"

Though she'd asked it in jest, Wade returned her smile with a serious look. "The day I fell in love with you."

She rested her palm against his cheek. "This is better than any movie I ever made," she assured him.

"It's better than any movie ever filmed," Wade said, then grinned. "Of course, so far I've only had a short course in Lauren Winters's films. Maybe my judgment's not so great."

"I think your judgment's just fine. You picked me, didn't you?"

Wade stroked a finger along the pale curve of her cheek. "I don't remember having any choice at all in the matter. You were just in my heart."

He glanced toward the house. "You fixed up a bedroom in that place yet?"

"Oh, yes. Despite Gina's pleas for me to do the kitchen first, I did the bedroom. I knew that was the first place you'd want to see."

"Smart woman," he said.

"The smartest," she agreed, and led him inside, where Wade spent the rest of the day proving just how clever—and lucky—they both were.

He'd just wrangled a Hollywood superstar into agreeing to marry him. Or had it been the other way around? He chuckled as he felt her hand slipping under the covers to slide up his leg. What difference did it make? This was clearly the life they'd both been destined for.

Epilogue

It was the strangest thing. Once she and Wade had agreed to get married, Lauren had been in no big hurry to arrange the ceremony. She'd had excuse after excuse, from the birth of Karen's baby to Gina's marriage to Rafe. The delay had driven Wade and the Calamity Janes crazy. They'd been pestering her for months now to set a date or to explain why she was so reluctant to stand in front of a minister and exchange vows with the man she loved.

The truth was, she had endured a media frenzy with her first two marriages. There was no way she wanted news of this wedding to leak out and turn a special, private moment into a circus. She had finally explained that to Wade, who'd come up with the perfect suggestion—a small wedding right here at their house with only friends and family in attendance. Even better, they hadn't even told the guests they were coming to a wedding, so there was no chance of an inadvertent leak. And they'd picked a date before Emma's due date, so they wouldn't steal that baby's thunder.

"Are you sure you're okay with all the secrecy?" Wade had asked a dozen times.

"I am deliriously happy with all the secrecy," she insisted.

"Gina's going to pitch a fit when she realizes you've flown a caterer in to do all the food," he pointed out.

"I couldn't very well have had her do it. Besides, she'll have other things to do. She and the other Calamity Janes are my bridesmaids." She frowned. "I just hope Emma isn't going to flip out at the dress I ordered for her. It is very difficult to find anything formal and flattering for a woman who is eight months pregnant."

"I thought bridesmaids almost always hated their dresses," he said. "Besides, I think she'll look fabulous. There is something about a pregnant woman...." His voice trailed off as his gaze wandered over her. "I can hardly wait."

"But wait you will, sweetie. We are not getting pregnant until after foaling season. I can't imagine what I was thinking planning a wedding for now. I'm so exhausted I can hardly see."

"Which is precisely why you are going inside, taking a long hot bath and going to bed," Wade countered. "I'll stay up with Miss Molly."

"But I want to be here when she has Midnight's foal," she protested. "It will be their first."

Wade hadn't even tried to argue with her, which was why she was running around frantically the next day an hour before their guests were due and two hours before the ceremony itself. Miss Molly's foal, a gorgeous colt, had been born just before dawn, which meant Lauren was operating on automatic pilot.

The kitchen was in chaos as the same Beverly Hills caterer who'd done Cassie's impromptu wedding two years earlier moaned and groaned about the outrageous miracles people expected of him.

"Just do it," Lauren ordered him. "I don't have time to pacify you. You can go back to L.A. and tell everyone that you know the reason that I left, that I am certifiably crazy."

Her offer put a gleam in his eye and he went back to putting the finishing touches on the elaborate wedding cake.

Lauren raced upstairs, showered and washed her hair and was just finishing her nails when the doorbell rang. Sighing, she put aside the polish and ran down to answer it. All four Calamity Janes simply stared.

"What?" she demanded.

"Are we early?" Gina asked.

"Exactly on time," Lauren said.

"Then why aren't you dressed?"

"Because I need a little help from my bridesmaids for that," she explained, laughing when they stared at her with openmouthed astonishment.

"Bridesmaids?" Emma said cautiously, her hand on her huge belly. "As in, you're getting married today?"

"Yep," Lauren confirmed, then grinned. "Surprise!"

Wade hadn't thought his life could get one bit sweeter, but that was before he stood in his own back-yard wearing a tuxedo and watching Lauren walk toward him looking like a princess. It was exactly the way he'd envisioned it, yards of white satin, a gossamer-sheer veil and all. He'd be lucky not to trip all over the vows, she made him so tongue-tied.

Which was nothing like what she'd done to his mother. He glanced at the small collection of chairs for the guests and winked at his mother when he caught her eye. She had been astonished when he had introduced her to Lauren. Turned out Arlene was one of Lauren's biggest fans, that she owned every one of Lauren's movies on video. She couldn't seem to get over the fact that her idol was actually marrying her son.

"Wait until I get home and tell everyone at the bar. They'll die. They'll absolutely die," she said.

"Actually, Mom, we've been thinking you might want to stick around here," he'd told her. "You don't need to work anymore. We have plenty of room. You can have your own house right here on the ranch."

Arlene had stared at him, perplexed. "But what would I do?"

"Nothing, unless you wanted to. You've earned the right to some time off."

She had waved off the suggestion. "Absolutely not. You're going to be newlyweds. I'm not about to be underfoot. We can discuss this after you have my first grandbaby."

Now she caught his gaze and winked back at him. Then Lauren was at his side, and he had eyes for nothing else.

From then on everything was a blur—the exchange of vows, the congratulations from the Calamity Janes and their spouses and Arlene. Wade's heart was too full to take any of it in. All he wanted to do was stare at his wife. *His wife!* He couldn't get over it.

"Oh, my."

Wade's gaze instantly shot to Emma. There had been no mistaking the alarm in her voice.

"You okay?" he asked, noting the pale cheeks, the near hysteria in her eyes.

Biting her lower lip, she shook her head. "I'm so sorry," she apologized.

"Sorry?" he asked, confused. "For what?"

"For upstaging your wedding. It seems I'm about to have a baby."

Wade stared at her. "Now? You're having the baby now?"

"Afraid so. Could you find Ford?"

"Absolutely, and I'll get Lauren right over here, too. I think she's inside."

Within an hour, the entire wedding party had moved to the hospital waiting room to the bemusement of the other waiting families.

Lauren sat by his side, her hand tucked in his. "Isn't it wonderful?" she said. "Emma's having her baby on our wedding day. I was so afraid we'd upstage her and now she's gone and done it to us."

"If you ask me, we should have predicted it," he teased.

"Why?"

"You are the Calamity Janes, aren't you? Isn't this just the kind of thing you do?"

A grin spread across her face. "You know, it is. And the most amazing thing is that you married me, anyway."

"Oh, darlin', it's a part of your charm. I wouldn't have you any other way. I imagine Rafe, Grady, Cole and Ford feel exactly the same way."

"Amen to that," Cole said, reaching for Cassie and

drawing her into his lap just as Rafe slipped his arms around Gina and Grady kissed Karen.

Just then Ford emerged from the delivery room. "It's a boy," he announced, looking dazed.

"A boy," Caitlyn said, looking disgusted. "I wanted a sister."

"I think having another boy around will be cool," Jake said. "With Aunt Karen's baby and my brother and now this one, there are more of us. Maybe we can grow up together and be just like you guys." He glanced at his mother. "We'll be the Calamity Johns."

"Absolutely not," Cassie told him. "This group is one of a kind."

Wade watched as she, Lauren, Gina and Karen gravitated together for a fierce hug. He glanced over at Cole and the other men.

"That group is one of a kind, no doubt about it," he said.

"No doubt at all," they agreed.

Rafe's grin spread. "And we're the lucky sons of guns who caught 'em."

Wade shook his head. "Sorry, pal. I'm a hundred percent certain it was the other way around. We never had a chance."

* * * * *

*And now turn the page
for a sneak preview of*

ASK ANYONE,

*the exciting new novel
by Sherryl Woods.
On sale in March 2002
from MIRA books.*

1

The God-blessed car was out of gas. Jenna pounded the steering wheel in frustration. Naturally her cell phone was dead. She'd used up the battery the night before trying to convince her daughter that it was absolutely not okay for her to dye her hair purple. She'd been so exhausted by the long distance battle that she hadn't thought to recharge the phone.

It was 9:52. She had exactly eight minutes to get to the yacht center. In her running shoes she might have been able to do it. In three-inch spike heels, she didn't have a prayer.

Maybe Bobby Spencer wasn't quite as much of a tight-ass as he'd seemed yesterday. Maybe she could be a few minutes late and still catch him. Yeah, right. The man had looked at her as if he'd rather be dealing with the devil. He'd obviously seize any excuse at all not to consider the Pennington and Sons proposal.

She stripped off her shoes, thanked heaven that her skirt had a slit in it and grabbed her briefcase off the seat. She hit the sidewalk at a dead run, grateful that she'd taken up jogging as a way to relieve stress.

It took her seven minutes and thirty seconds to reach the yacht center. She had runs in her hose, blisters on her feet and her hair no doubt looked as if it had been styled in a wind tunnel, but she was on time.

Bobby Spencer, however, was late.

Jenna stared at the secretary. "He's not here," she repeated incredulously.

"Never gets in before eleven," the woman said, clearly working to contain her curiosity over Jenna's disheveled appearance.

Jenna's temper, which she usually worked really, really hard to contain, began to simmer. "Never," she echoed.

"Not that I can recall," the woman said. "He works late at night. Besides, he's just not a morning person. Believe me, you don't want to see him at this hour."

"Look…what's your name?"

"Maggie."

"Okay, Maggie, here's the thing. I saw Mr. Spencer yesterday. He told me to be here at ten. He made a really big deal bout it. My car broke down, but I busted my butt to be on time. Could you get on that phone and track him down and tell him that I'm here and getting more pissed by the minute that he's not?"

Maggie grinned.

Jenna sighed. "Okay, you can leave out the part about my attitude."

"Maybe you could think of this as a blessing in disguise," Maggie said. "You know, use the time to kind of put yourself back together. Not that appearances are everything, but you look kinda like you tangled with a wrestler or something. I've got a sewing kit right here I could loan you.''

Jenna stared at her blankly. ''A sewing kit?''

''Your skirt,'' she said, then gestured. ''And your jacket.''

Jenna looked down. The slit in her skirt now extended almost to the waistband. Two buttons on her jacket were hanging by threads, which left a gaping space across her chest featuring an ample display of skin and lace.

''Oh, God,'' she murmured.

''Now don't get upset,'' Maggie said, bouncing up at once. She rummaged in her desk. ''Here's the sewing kit.'' She glanced worriedly from the array of tiny spools of thread to Jenna's outfit, then grabbed the stapler. ''Come with me. We'll have you fixed up in no time. It might not be pretty, but you will be decent.''

''What if Mr. Spencer comes while you're away from your desk?''

''Oh, don't worry about Bobby. He's a sweetie once he's had his coffee.''

''Really?'' Jenna regarded her skeptically as Maggie led the way into a nearby bathroom. She stripped off her clothes and they went to work.

''Oh, sure. Everyone knows that. Everybody in town loves Bobby.'' She grinned at Jenna. ''I heard about the commotion at his house yesterday. I would have given anything to be there to see his face.''

''Actually he looked a little ticked,'' Jenna confided as Maggie stitched and stapled her skirt back together, while she worked on the buttons on her jacket.

''To tell you the truth, that's a good thing. We've all been saying for a long time now that somebody needs to come along and shake up that man's life. He's in a rut, emotionally speaking, that is.''

Jenna didn't give two figs what kind of a rut the man was in. She wanted to sell him on this proposal and get out of town with a signed contract in hand.

Only after her clothes were mended as well as they could be did Jenna risk a look in the mirror. Her cheeks were still flushed. Her hair, which had started the day in a nice, neat french twist, was hanging down around her shoulders in a tangle of untamed curls.

Of course, the image reflected back at her wasn't nearly as disconcerting as the image of Bobby Spencer's stunned expression right next to it.

A half-dressed Jenna Kennedy was standing in *his* private bathroom. Bobby reluctantly dragged his gaze from full breasts barely covered with scraps of lace to her startled face.

''Seen enough?'' she snapped.

He blinked. ''Sorry,'' he said, then shut the door. ''Maggie, get out here!''

His secretary emerged from the bathroom. ''What the hell is going on?'' he demanded.

''Long story, boss. Jenna will be out in a minute. She can explain. I've got work to do.''

He shook his head. ''Since when are you anxious to get to work?''

''Since five seconds ago,'' she said with an unrepentant grin. ''Go easy on her. She's had a rough morning.''

Bobby sighed. ''I'm not in the habit of terrorizing people.''

''You know that and I know that,'' Maggie agreed. ''She doesn't seem to be so sure. Why is that?''

"Never mind. Go to work."

"I made coffee," she said.

Bobby shuddered. "I know. From now on, leave that to me. Yours tastes like axle grease."

He walked through the yacht center to the restaurant kitchen, prepared a decent pot of coffee, poured two cups, then took them back to his office and sat behind his desk. Jenna still hadn't emerged from his bathroom. He alternately checked his watch and gazed warily at the door as if a restless tiger might be lurking behind it. Finally the knob turned and his pulse kicked up a notch. He deliberately attributed it to annoyance at her tardiness, because anything else was unacceptable.

"You're late," he said, just to emphasize his displeasure.

"No," she said just as emphatically. "I was right on time. Imagine my surprise when I was told that you *never* come in before eleven. If I'd known that, I could have found a better way to get here than running all the way."

He stared. "You ran? Why?"

"My car ran out of gas. Because you made such a big deal about me being on time, I got out, took off my shoes, hiked up my skirt and ran, which is why you found me in your bathroom looking like a complete wreck."

"I see." A dozen questions came to mind, along with quite a few disconcerting images. He would have paid money to see her cross-town race to get here. In fact, he was surprised he hadn't heard about it from someone by now.

She eyed him warily. "That's all you have to say?"

"I'm sorry," he said. "You could have called and explained."

She shook her head. "My cell phone was dead." As if she realized she was making a less than stellar impression, she drew in a deep breath and said, "Maybe we should just get straight to my ideas for your boardwalk development."

Bobby sighed. "Sure. Why not?" Listening didn't mean he had to agree to anything.

But as Jenna talked, he began to see a revitalized area along the riverfront that would be absolutely perfect for Trinity Harbor.

"I assume the centerpiece would be an antique carousel," he said.

She blinked as if he'd pulled the idea out of thin air. "How did you know?"

"That horse you sent was a definite clue," he said. "Thank heavens, it's out of my front yard, though."

Her mouth dropped open. "It's gone?"

"Since last night," he said, watching worriedly as her skin turned pale. "You had it picked up, didn't you?"

She shook her head. "What happened to the guard? I paid him to stay right there with it."

"I have no idea. He was gone when I got home, too." He studied her stricken expression. "Are you telling me that someone stole that horse?"

Jenna nodded. "Oh, God," she murmured. "My father is right. I am the world's worst screwup. That horse is worth a fortune. And the rest of the carousel won't be worth all that much without it."

Her plaintive tone struck a responsive note somewhere deep inside Bobby. He knew a whole lot about judgmental fathers. "Insurance?" he suggested hopefully.

She shook her head. "The guard was cheaper. I used

every last penny of my savings to buy that carousel and hire the guard to watch over the horse for the day.''

Bobby reached for the phone. ''I'll get Tucker over here,'' he said grimly. He wanted that antique carousel horse found and found fast, because the protective feelings that Jenna Kennedy stirred in him had trouble written all over them.

When California's most talked about dynasty is threatened, only family, privilege and the power of love can protect them!

THE COLTONS

Coming in November 2001

PASSION'S LAW

by

Ruth Langan

Hard-boiled police detective Thaddeus Law had only one mission: catch the son of a gun out to kill Joe Colton. And his objective would be more easily attained if beautiful heiress Heather McGrath would stay out of his way. Besides, the only princess in Thad's life was his two-year-old daughter. But were Heather's suggestive glances telling him otherwise?

Available at your favorite retail outlet.

Silhouette ®

Where love comes alive ™

THE F RTUNES OF TEXAS

invite you to a memorable Christmas celebration in

Gifts of FORTUNE

Patriarch Ryan Fortune has met death head-on
and now he has a special gift for each of the four
honorable individuals who stood by him in his hour
of need. This holiday collection contains stories
by three of your most beloved authors.

THE HOLIDAY HEIR
by Barbara Boswell

THE CHRISTMAS HOUSE
by Jennifer Greene

MAGGIE'S MIRACLE
by Jackie Merritt

And be sure to watch for **Did You Say Twins?!** by
Maureen Child, the exciting conclusion to the
Fortunes of Texas: The Lost Heirs miniseries,
coming only to Silhouette Desire in December 2001.

*Don't miss these unforgettable romances…
available at your favorite retail outlet.*

Silhouette®
Where love comes alive™

This November 2001—
Silhouette Books cordially invites you
to the wedding of two of our favorite

YULETIDE BRIDES

A woman gets stuck faking happily-ever-after with her soon-to-be ex-husband—or *is* she faking?—all the while hiding their baby-to-be, in **Marie Ferrarella's CHRISTMAS BRIDE.**

A man hired to bring back a mogul's lost granddaughter goes from daring detective to darling dad, when he falls for the girl *and* her adoptive mother, in **Suzanne Carey's FATHER BY MARRIAGE.**

Because there's nothing like
a Christmas wedding...

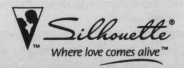

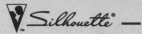